Relyk

Robert A Palmer

Eva K Palmer

Copyright © 2013 Robert A Palmer

Published by
Skowndral Hill Publishers
Sioux Falls, SD 57107

First Edition: August 2013

Robertpalmerbooks.com

ISBN: 1490981225
ISBN-13: 978-1490981222

DEDICATION

To all the people in our lives that help us make our
dreams come true.

CONTENTS

ACKNOWLEDGMENTS

I would like to thank my parents and grandparents, who taught me in my childhood the history that made this idea possible.

I would also like to thank my daughter for her countless ideas and vivid imagination that made this story even better than the original version.

PALMER

PROLOGUE

The giant, hulking king sat at the head of his table, grease dribbling down his chin and forearm from the turkey leg clenched in his fleshy grip. He chewed slowly, thoughtfully, before taking another massive bite and dropping the hunk of flesh to the table. A stiff breeze drifted in from outside, ruffling the bottom of the tent and sending a small swirl of sand across the tent floor. The cool evening air calmed the fire burning in his heart. Voices from outside floated in on the wind, along with the sound of footsteps quickly approaching.

The door of the tent opened slowly and the face of his personal servant appeared in the doorway, lit dimly by the candles inside the tent. The hulk-king remained deep in thought, staring intently at the table, seemingly ignoring the servant's presence.

"Have you located it?" the king asked finally, his gravelly voice, weary yet forceful, echoing off the wooden table top.

"Yes my lord," the servant replied, bowing deeply. "It's in the temple."

The king wiped the grease from his chin and snorted gruffly. "Of course it is. Their tradition makes them weak...predictable. Their absurd dependence on their rituals will be their undoing." He stood and crossed the tent to his armor that hung from pegs attached to one of the support poles in the middle of the tent. "Where is my wife?"

"She's with her bodyguards, my lord."

"And my son?"

"He is with his mother."

"Bring him to me."

The servant bowed stiffly and backed quickly out of the tent. The king listened as his footsteps retreated in the direction from which they'd come. When they'd finally silenced, he turned back to his armor, strapping on his breast plate and cinching it up tight. He exhaled deeply, slowing his breathing and his heart rate as he watched the gleam of the candlelight flicker and dance across the face of his armor. While he did not anticipate much of a fight, his heart still raced with adrenaline. After years of dealing with these problematic people, he would finally crush them once in for all. His thoughts turned to the years of war leading to this moment; the people lost, the energy expended. It all ended tonight. The rapidly returning footsteps invaded his thoughts and he turned to the door.

The king's son exploded into the tent, followed closely by the bowing servant. He was dressed in full battle garb; breast plate, sandals, belt, and cloak, with his shield and spear attached to his back. His sword hung at his side, steadied by his firm grip on its hilt. The king took in the vision of youthful exuberance, but did not address his son immediately. Instead, he met his son's eyes and held his gaze for several tense moments.

Finally he spoke. "Embrace me, my son," the king said as he thrust an enormous, muscled hand in the younger man's direction.

The prince took a quick yet apprehensive step forward, gripping his father's forearm as the elder did the same to his son.

"Every nation I've conquered, every people I've subdued, every army I've defeated, has been to build an empire for you to someday rule." He stared deeply into his son's eyes searching for any measure of fear. He found none. "Tonight, you seize your birthright."

He clapped his son on the shoulder and turned to the servant. "Prepare my guards. My son and I will lead them to the temple to retrieve the idol."

"What of the city, my lord?" the servant replied, head bowed facing the ground.

"When we have the idol, burn it to the ground," he hissed. "Wipe their miserable existence from the history of the earth."

I

The sun peeked over a craggy ridge, spreading its rays across the sleepy town of Hill City as early morning dawned in the Black Hills. A light breeze floated through an open window, producing goose bumps on the exposed arms of Sheriff Maddie Turner, and causing her to stir slightly in her bed. Light was beginning to pour in through every available opening, and if there was one thing certain to coax her out of bed at this time of day, it was a brilliant South Dakota sunrise. She sat up squinting, rubbing her dreams out of her large brown eyes, and running her hands through her dark, shoulder-length hair.

She showered and dressed quickly, grabbing an apple and a granola bar from the lazy susan as she headed out the door. Her elderly friends, Marvin and Roda Johnson had just returned from a two week vacation in Europe the night before, and she was anxious to hear all about it. As excited as she was to see them, and catch up over a game of cards, she had promised to wait until the next day as they were sure to be tired from their long flight.

She left town and pointed her truck east in the direction of Mitchell Lake and the Johnsons' home. The sun had breached the valley's walls and was washing the basin in light as she pulled into their drive. Birds searching for an early breakfast chirped and scuttled away to announce her arrival. The cool morning air kissed the back of her neck as she stepped out of her pickup and onto the gravel driveway that edged along the small lake. She stood still for a moment, gulping in the smell of the pine trees and basking in the morning sun. It was going to be a gorgeous day.

She bounced up the steps and knocked firmly on the door, which gave way under the pressure and slowly creaked open. She furrowed her brow questioningly as she poked her head through the doorway and looked around. It wasn't unusual for the Johnsons to leave their door open, but Maddie was surprised it was unlocked at this early hour. Roda knew she was coming though, she thought to herself as she stepped through the doorway and into the front hall.

"Hello?" she called out quietly. "Are you guys in here, or are you down at the lake?" She paused momentarily thinking inwardly. "Am I talking to myself?" she said smiling and rounding the corner into the living room. She stopped cold and her smile vanished.

Marvin sat in his recliner just ahead of her facing the TV, but he wasn't moving a muscle. His mouth hung open loosely and his eyes fixed on a point well beyond the front of the television set that was playing quietly. At the base of his chair lay a coffee mug tipped on its side; its contents oozing a dark stain across the thick shag carpet. He was fully clothed, but from the looks of the stain in the carpet, he'd been sitting there a while. It looked to Maddie like he hadn't even made it to his bed from the night before.

She looked quickly from side to side, but nothing else seemed out of the ordinary. No signs of a struggle were evident, but Roda was nowhere to be found. A flash of movement caught her attention through the window and she stepped to her side to get a better view. Instinctively, she reached to her side and cursed herself for not bringing her gun. Slowly, she peeled a corner of the lace curtains back to reveal the hind end of a deer bounding away into the woods.

She exhaled slowly and shook her head at herself before turning her attention back to Marvin. She approached his body slowly, careful not to disturb whatever evidence might be present. She stepped to his side and eyed his face thoughtfully, not even bothering to check for a pulse. From the lack of color in his skin, and the amount of time he'd obviously been sitting there, it was clear he was deceased. She ran a hand sideways over his head, patting down a clump of tousled hair. A tear streaked down her cheek and she wiped it away quickly with a sniffle for emphasis.

She looked up in the direction of the second floor and took a deep breath. "Roda?" her voice cracked as she called out loudly. "Are you up there?"

Why wouldn't she be here, and why wouldn't she have called me? Maddie thought to herself as she rounded the corner to the stairs and headed up. The question continued to nag at her as she searched the entire second floor to no avail. Their suitcases sat upright at the foot of their bed, evidence they hadn't even gotten around to unpacking yet. Nothing else seemed out of place.

She headed back downstairs, and as she did, she dialed Roda's number on her cell phone. She waited only moments before a chirp erupted from the kitchen. She followed the noise to find the phone lying abandoned on the kitchen table. She stood staring at the device as it sang to her, lost in thought. Finally she pressed the button on her phone to end the call, and the serenade died.

Before replacing the phone in her back pocket, she dialed a second number.

"Coroner's office, this is John," came the overly cheery voice on the other end.

"Hi John, this is Maddie." She choked back tears as her throat began to burn. "I'm out at the Johnsons' house, and Marvin is dead. Can you come out right away?"

"Oh, Maddie I'm so sorry," John said, understanding full well the bond she shared with the elderly couple. "Didn't they just get back from Europe? How's Roda doing?"

"I'm not sure yet," she said, ignoring the first question. "I can't find her anywhere."

"I'll be right over," John said, not wasting any time.

"Thanks," Maddie replied quietly as she hit the button to end the call.

She put her phone back in the pocket she'd retrieved it from, keeping it close. Her head snapped up and she stood staring out the kitchen window at the bright, morning sun. Stepping away from the sink, she exited the home the way she'd come in through the front door, kissing Marvin lightly on his head as she passed. She stood on the front porch surveying the yard before circling the property twice, looking for anything that would help her discover the whereabouts of her friend Roda.

Adopted by a single father as a small child, Maddie had never really known a mother. She was a self-proclaimed tomboy, who preferred fixing her truck to romantic comedies. When she graduated high school, her father had given her a brand new Toyota Tacoma, and she had kept it running ever since. But when the

Johnsons had come into her life, she had been drawn to Roda in a way only a motherless woman could be. They accepted her almost as their own flesh and blood, and she was grateful to finally have that missing piece of the puzzle filled in. She knew someday that happiness would be threatened, but she wasn't ready for it yet.

She slowed to a stop, and buckled to the ground under the weight of her sorrow. She sat on her knees for several moments, sobbing uncontrollably into her hands. She knew she had a job to do, and John would be arriving any second, but for the time being, she didn't care. Her thoughts drifted to the long conversations over games of canasta, late night fire pits, and their many walks through the wooded area around the lake. Eventually she turned her mind to Roda and doubts of her friend's safety rose up overwhelmingly, bringing with them a fresh round of tears. She did not know how long she knelt there, but finally the sobs subsided and she wiped at her eyes with the hem of her tank top. As she let out one loud, final sniffle, John's car pulled into the drive and made a slow turn in the circular driveway.

She came to her feet as he stepped out of his vehicle to greet her. The look of compassion in his eyes tugged at her heart and threatened to spiral her back into hopeless weeping, but she fought it back. She reached out a hand to shake his, but he sidestepped it and hugged her tight. It was unexpected, but not unwelcome.

"I'm so sorry, Maddie," he said quietly, squeezing her tightly.

She'd known John Bauer for almost fifteen years, and as the sheriff, she'd worked with him on multiple occasions. She'd seen him interact with families, but this was the first time she'd been on the receiving end. His compassion was sincere. If she hadn't just finished crying, she would have opened the floodgates on his shoulder. It was no surprise everyone in town liked him even though most people only talked to him when death visited their families.

They stood that way for several moments before Maddie finally pulled away and straightened herself.

"Thanks for coming out so quickly," she said turning away and tilting her head toward the house. "Marvin is in the living room, in his recliner. I still haven't found Roda, and I can't imagine she would have left him like that without calling. I just don't know where she would be." She paused but then added quietly, "I'm assuming the worst. Hopefully I'm wrong."

John looked at her knowingly. "Any idea what caused it? Any reason to think it was anything other than natural causes?"

Maddie shook her head resolutely. "No foul play from what I could see," she replied quietly. "He looks…peaceful. Something about this just doesn't seem right though. My gut tells me it wasn't exactly natural."

John squinted at her comment, but let it pass. "I'll get to work," he said, before turning back to his vehicle to get his equipment.

Two steps back toward his car, his footsteps on the gravel stopped abruptly. Maddie had looked away, but the sudden end to the noise drew her attention back. She wheeled around, looking at John, who was staring over the ridge to the south. Just over the crest sat a footbridge that spanned a small inlet feeding the lake. He rose up on his tip-toes to get a better view, and then suddenly took off at a full sprint toward the bridge.

"Roda!" he yelled loudly, as Maddie's eyes widened and she took off after him.

They reached the bridge at a full sprint and clambered onto it, their force rocking the small wooden crosswalk as they came to a halt. Maddie knelt down next to Roda, who was slumped in a heap with her face resting against the wooden treads.

Her skin was a pale gray and cold to the touch. Dark bruises discolored the bottom half of her face where blood had already begun to pool. She looked just like Marvin did. There were no wounds, no signs of a struggle at all. It was as if she had just dropped dead on the bridge. She was fully dressed, and the cool dampness that permeated her clothes suggested she'd been there all night, with only the morning dew for company. In one tightly closed fist, she held the handkerchief that Maddie had given to Marvin a couple years ago as a joke. It had turned into one of his favored possessions.

Despite her earlier tears, Maddie's body found a way to produce more. She rested her hand on Roda's lifeless shoulder as a fresh dose of saltwater washed down her cheeks and across her lips.

John touched her shoulder lightly as he rose to his feet. "I'll start in the house," he said quietly and turned and walked away.

Maddie lowered her head to Roda's shoulder, once again allowing the sobs to wash over her body. Even through closed eyes, her tears forced their way down her cheeks to her friend's shirt sleeve. She rested there for what felt like an eternity, consenting to her sorrow. Finally, she lifted her head and allowed the morning sun to dab at her tear-soaked cheeks.

The small lake lay at the foot of a large rock formation. At the farthest shore, the stone rose vertically, setting the pool in a gorgeous backdrop that always put Maddie at ease. It was not working today, and she feared the view would forever be stained by the events of this morning.

She looked down at Roda's face trying to imagine what could have possibly happened to her friends. Roda's eyes were still open and pointed toward the lake, just like Marvin. And just like Marvin, she was the picture of peace and serenity. Maddie wiped one final tear away and reached down and closed Roda's eyes. She kissed her lightly on her forehead before standing up and walking back toward the house. She reached the front steps just as John was exiting through the front door.

"I didn't see anything out of the ordinary," John said, removing his glasses and wiping them on the hem of his shirt. "My first guess would be heart attack, but with Roda out there..." he gestured toward the footbridge as he trailed off, searching for words. Finally he gave up and stated the obvious. "We're going to have to perform an autopsy."

Maddie was staring absently at the porch floor and nodded her head slightly at the words. She heard what he said, but her brain wasn't really processing anymore. She wanted to know what happened, but didn't know if she could handle all the details at the moment. She just needed a moment alone. Finally, she looked up at John and realized she'd been zoning out and he was still talking.

"...get a guy up here and help me take the bodies back into town," he said, apparently finishing up his sentence.

"Thanks John," she said, nodding her head and shaking his hand. She hoped he hadn't asked her something that she was ignoring, or that she had just agreed to something she wasn't aware of. By the look on his face, everything appeared to be business as usual. "I'm going to head back to the office and fill out my report. I'll send one of the other guys up to help you."

John nodded slightly, but didn't give any indication that her response was out of line. "I'll call when I have the autopsy results," he replied. "See you back in town."

She turned and headed back to her truck. As she opened the door, she paused to stare one last time over the small embankment at the wooden structure that was now Roda's final resting place. Over the ridge, she could just see the top half of Roda's shoulder against the backdrop of the lake. A single tear slipped down her cheek and stopped just above her lips. She wiped it away, sat down in the driver's seat, and pointed the vehicle back toward home. She needed to get her gun and uniform from the house. It looked like she'd be working today after all.

II

On a normal day, Maddie would have taken the bypass back to her house and avoided the congestion of the multiple intersections through the heart of the little town. But today, she was lost in thought and didn't make her usual turn. She didn't even realize what she'd done until she was half way down Main Street.

Tourists roamed the sidewalks, venturing in and out of the little shops that lined the street on either side, searching for that one special souvenir that would make the whole trip memorable. She listened distractedly at the chatter of voices and the roar of engines as motorcycles filled parking spots, alleys, and any empty nook they could find. Early rally-goers were already flooding the area even though none of the scheduled events would be getting underway for a few more days.

The Sturgis Motorcycle Rally was one of the biggest rallies in the world and it attracted riders from all over the country. Over the next fourteen days, half a million thirsty bikers would descend on an area that normally held 100,000 people. The entire Black Hills would be infested with the small vehicles and their partying riders, making everyday activities almost intolerable. Even though the bulk of the festivities took place fifty miles to the north, the event would keep her plenty busy. It sure was good for the economy though.

As she passed the south end of Main Street, the diner came into view and she remembered she was supposed to meet her dad for lunch at eleven. With the events of the morning, she'd completely forgotten about the appointment. She looked at the clock on her dashboard. 10:12. She needed the time with her father more than ever, but with paperwork to fill out, she was going to be late. She snapped the phone to her ear and punched her father's number. After two rings, he picked up.

"Hey Sunshine," he said cheerily.

His voice almost sent her back into tears. "Hi Dad," she said, her voice cracking. "Say, I was calling about our lunch date."

"You're not standing me up, are you?" he said jokingly. "I've had this circled on my calendar all week."

She smiled at the thought. Her father, an ex-FBI agent, had a memory like a steel trap and enough organizational skills to overwhelm a secretary on Ritalin. He didn't even need a calendar, and he certainly didn't need one to remember lunch with his daughter.

"No, but something came up," she said, choking back a tear. Through her friendship, her father had also become friends with the Johnsons, and they had spent countless hours together. While she badly wanted to talk about it, she didn't have the heart to tell him over the phone. He must have sensed her uneasiness.

"Is everything ok, honey?" he asked, sympathy creeping into his voice.

"It will be, but I don't want to talk about it over the phone," she said hurriedly. "I'll tell you everything at lunch. I have to fill out some paperwork, so I wanted to see if we could push back lunch a little. Would noon be ok?" In his professional life, paperwork had been half of his job description. She knew he'd understand.

"Absolutely," he replied. "I've got a couple errands to run downtown anyway. How's the biker situation? Is it a full infestation yet?"

Maddie stifled a laugh. He always had a way of cheering her up. "Nothing a little pepper spray can't handle," she said chuckling.

"See you at noon, Sweetheart," her dad said before hanging up.

As she finished her drive, her thoughts stayed on her father. When she was just a child, her mother had gone to prison for the murder of her biological father. Two years later, she died of cancer in a prison cell. She'd never seen her mother after her arrest. The man she now called father, Anthony Turner, had been the FBI agent assigned to investigate her parents due to their involvement in organized crime in the south. When her mother was imprisoned, he took her in as his own and they moved to South Dakota. They never looked back. Like her adopted father, she had chosen the path of law enforcement, and she thanked God every day for the life he'd given her; a life she knew she never would have had with her biological parents.

After collecting her uniform from home, she made the return trip through downtown, wrinkling her nose in frustration at the growing bottleneck. Reaching the station, she stepped out into the hot sun and sighed heavily. Even in the morning, July in that area could coax a sweat out of just about anyone, and the recently-donned uniform wasn't helping matters.

As she walked to the door, it quickly swung open and Frank Hester, the resident Game Warden, bounded out with a smile. He shouted something inaudible over his shoulder and then laughed out loud at the response as he strode into the parking lot. He was a heavy set man who enthusiastically embraced and relished the 'jolly fat man' label. Maddie couldn't remember the last time she'd seen him without a smile on his face.

"Maddie!" he said loudly when he noticed her approaching. She couldn't help but smile, in spite of herself.

"How are you, Frank?" she said as he put up his hand for a high five. She slapped his hand half-heartedly which drew a face of mock ire. He raised his hand again and this time she slapped it so hard it made her wince.

"What's the good word, Sheriff?" he asked finally.

"Not a good word, but two deceased up at Mitchell Lake," she said sadly.

"Two?" he asked. She picked up on the unspoken part of the question.

"Both look to be natural causes." She paused, fighting back a tear yet again. "It was the Johnsons. Bauer's up there now. I'm sending one of my guys to help."

This news brought a frown to Frank's face. "I'm sorry, Maddie," he said, putting a hand on her shoulder to offer his condolences. She knew everyone had good intentions, and it was the right thing to say in that situation, but she was getting tired of hearing that phrase already.

"That's part of life, right?" she said, shrugging and looking back up at him. Another tear escaped the confinement of her eyelids and streaked down her cheek. She brushed it away as quickly as it appeared.

"I'm actually headed up that direction now," Frank finally said, breaking the silence.

"Why's that?"

"I guess some kids found a bunch of dead fish washed up on the creek shore just under the mouth of the stream. I didn't hear any explosions up there last night, did you?" he asked, a joking smile crossing his lips.

Fishermen looking to cheat the system would occasionally throw dynamite into a lake to force the fish to the surface. After that, it was a simple matter of collecting them with a net. Sometimes whole schools of fish died in the process. It didn't happen much anymore, and certainly not in a canyon where the echo from the explosion would be loud enough to wake a deaf man, but she knew what he was getting at. She snorted a small laugh and shook her head.

"Sounds like fun," she said sarcastically giving him a half-hearted smile as he strode away.

"Tell everyone to come to my place tonight," he called loudly as he stepped into his vehicle. "We'll have a fish fry!" His laugh was cut short by the slamming of his door, but Maddie could see him smiling to himself as he pulled out of the parking lot.

She waved a hand at him as she chuckled and headed through the station doors. She blinked hard as her eyes adjusted to the darker environment. Billy Murphy, one of her deputies was seated at the desk near the entryway.

"Is Frank still outside?" he asked quickly as he began to stand.

"He was just driving away. Why?" she asked as the air conditioning kicked on behind her, tickling her neck and sending a shiver down her spine.

"He left his sunglasses on the desk," he replied, holding them aloft like he'd just found the Holy Grail.

"Well, you can take them up to him on your way to Mitchell Lake."

He raised his eyebrows questioningly.

"No, you're not getting a day off," she said quickly. "Marvin and Roda Johnson passed away last night. Bauer's up there and I told him I'd send someone to help him. It's your lucky day."

Billy's face fell instantly. "I'm sorry, boss," he offered somewhat weakly.

No tears this time. She'd had enough of the sympathy already. "Thank you," she replied, blinking involuntarily and nodding at him curtly. "I've got some paperwork to do. I'll watch the station until Brody gets here at noon."

She didn't need to ask him twice. She'd barely gotten the words out when he bounded around his desk and grabbed the keys to one of the cruisers from the wall. Youthful exuberance was clearly more excited about going out in the heat than she was. She shook her head as she stepped into her office and seated herself at the computer.

******

Ninety minutes later, she was putting the final touches on her report as her other deputy, Brody Franklin strode in through the front door. With less than half a year of experience, Brody was the newest member of the department. After high school, he'd enlisted and spent several years in Afghanistan learning networking, telecommunications, and programming skills. The locals all said he was a nice kid growing up; happy, respectful, and kind. He was still respectful, but his time in the military must have driven the happiness out of him. He was a little more serious than she would have liked, rarely showing emotion, but he was good at his job. And with his networking skills, courtesy of Uncle Sam, he was their resident helpdesk. He paused at her door, clearly not expecting to see her today.

"I thought you were off today," he said matter-of-factly as he double-checked the calendar on the wall.

"A couple things came up," she replied before filling him in on the morning's events. He had known the Johnsons fairly well also, so she thought he would take it harder than Billy. It barely seemed to register with him.

"That's too bad," he said while staring through the floor. "They were always nice to me when I was a kid. Do you need me to do anything?"

"Just keep an eye on the station until Billy gets back. I'm heading to lunch and don't plan on being back today."

He backed out of her office and circled to the front desk. "Will do!" he said loudly as he plopped down hard.

Maddie saved her work and nodded to Brody as she passed him on her way out. She caught a glimpse of his screen as she passed. He was surfing some techy message board. She just smiled and nodded as she exited the building and stepped into her truck.

She made the short trip quickly, even with Main Street becoming rapidly overcrowded. At 12:03, she stepped into the diner to be greeted by the overpowering aroma of fried food, grease, and chocolate. The neon lights above the counter glowed faintly, beckoning her warmly to come in and make herself comfortable.

Scanning the restaurant, she found her father at the counter, already half a straw deep into a large chocolate shake, complete with whipped cream and a cherry. In his own mind, her father was a legendary cheeseburger and milkshake aficionado, and this place made some of the best. It was, by far, one of their favorite places to eat.

He caught her reflection in the large mirror that adorned the front, and turned quickly, smiling and waving her over. She walked toward him, shaking her head and smiling to herself.

"Hi, Honey," he said standing up and giving her a hug. He'd just been over two days earlier to help fix some deck boards, but after the day she was having, it seemed like an eternity since she'd seen him. She held the hug just a little longer than usual. Several more tears dripped from her tightly-closed lids and as she backed away, she realized she'd dampened the front of her father's shirt. He noticed, but didn't seem to care.

"So what's going on?" he asked, sitting down on his stool and motioning for her to sit at the stool next to his.

"I went up to the lake to see Marvin and Roda this morning," she started slowly, keeping her voice in check.

"Are they ok?" her father asked hesitantly.

She shook her head, her voice betraying her again. She cleared her throat and finally found the words. "When I got up there, they were both dead."

"What?!?" he said, more loudly than he had intended. Several of the patrons in the restaurant stopped their conversations and looked in their direction. He smiled sheepishly and turned back to Maddie. "What happened? Was it a robbery? Was it those bikers?" He cursed under his breath and looked absently around the restaurant.

His questions and comments were coming rapid fire and she couldn't keep up with them all. The unintended consequence of his career was that her father still saw shadows around every corner. She couldn't say that she blamed him, but she wanted to keep this as low-key as possible.

"Dad!" she said sternly, waving her hands in the air to get his attention. "It wasn't anything like that."

He stopped talking immediately and looked directly into her eyes.

"They were just...dead," she said finally. "Marvin was sitting in his chair facing the TV. Roda was out lying on the footbridge. Nothing was out of place and there were no signs of a struggle. They were both healthy. I just don't get it." She trailed off and stared at the countertop, lost in thought. Her father didn't say a word, and she didn't have the strength at the moment to make eye contact again. Despite his stormy background, he had the kindest eyes she had ever seen. Looking into them now would surely turn her to a sniveling puddle of tears.

Finally, she found the words to continue. "John's bringing their bodies back to town to perform an autopsy. I sent Billy up there because I don't think I would have been much help."

Her father placed a comforting hand on her shoulder. "I'm sure there's a logical explanation, and if anyone can find it, it's you and John."

She flashed a small smile behind the hair that hung around her face. He was right. John would be able to tell her what happened.

A loud cough from one of the patrons in the corner brought her back to the present and she lifted her head to look at her father. He was smiling sympathetically at her. So caught up in her own sorrow had she been until now, that she didn't even stop to think how her father was feeling. They had been his friends too.

"Sorry, Dad," she said suddenly. "I didn't want to tell you this over the phone. I thought it was better in person." It was her way of offering an apology of sorts. He understood what she was getting at.

"Don't worry about your old dad," he said smiling. "I will miss them a lot, but I've been through much worse. I'll be ok." He stopped for a moment and looked down at the counter. "Do you still want to eat?"

The coughing from the corner was becoming more and more pronounced, and both of them turned their attention in that direction for a moment. Three men sat at a corner booth, and one of them was clearly having a difficult time with his meal. Maddie turned back to her father and shrugged, just as the waitress arrived to take their orders.

Their server wore a dress reminiscent of the fifties, a dirty apron wrapped tightly around her waist, and a name tag with a hand-written label that read 'Flo'.

Anthony squinted at the name tag and then looked up at the waitress.

"Janet, that thing doesn't seriously work, does it?" he asked in disbelief.

"It sure does, Sugar," the waitress replied, giving him a wink and a wide smile. "Tourists wander in here looking for the full diner experience, and that includes a waitress named Flo. I have to live off these tips during the offseason, you know!"

Anthony just shook his head and chuckled under his breath. The monetary feast of the tourist season was starkly offset by the famine of winter, when the influx of money dried up and only the locals and a few skiers remained to support the small economy. Leave it to some of the more seasoned veterans to figure out how to squeeze every last drop of money out of the busy times.

"What can I get for you two today?" she asked cheerily.

"Not what he's having," her father joked, tilting his thumb in the direction of the corner.

Janet rolled her eyes with annoyance. "Those three yahoos just walked in before you two did. They're tired, drunk, hungry, and obnoxious all rolled into one."

Maddie perked up at the mention of drinking. "Did they drive here drunk?" she asked quietly.

"I would assume so, Darlin'," she replied. "Apparently they were up just under the Mitchell Lake outlet, fishing since early this morning. More drinking than fishing if you ask me," she finished with a head shake of disapproval as she pulled her pen from her pocket preparing to take their order.

"Well, there's a reason they call it fishing and not catching," Anthony offered, laughing at the thought of fishermen having to eat at a diner and not what they caught themselves.

As he spoke, Maddie turned to look at the three men again. Just then, the coughing man kicked things up a notch. He was coughing loudly, trying to clear his throat, and looking positively uncomfortable. His friends, while displaying concern for his condition, didn't look to be in much better shape. The man in the corner of the booth was covered in welts like he'd wandered through an entire field of poison ivy. Maddie hadn't noticed it before, but now that she was getting a closer look, it was plainly visible. The third man had his back to them, but from the discoloration on his shirt, she could tell he was sweating profusely. He teetered in his seat while watching the man cough himself silly.

"Something's not quite right over there," her father said quietly from behind her.

The waitress, who had been staring at her notepad waiting for an order, finally looked up to see them both glaring toward the corner. She followed their gaze just as the coughing man was rising to his feet. Maddie and her father rose to their feet as well, ready to act if necessary.

With one loud, final cough, the man wobbled on his feet like a boxer who'd been through fifteen rounds. He spun a quarter turn, facing directly toward them, and raised a hand in their direction as if pleading for help. His face was as white as a sheet and panic was clearly in control at the moment. Maddie began moving in his direction, her father close on her heels. Suddenly, the man's eyes rolled back in his head and his knees buckled like a cheap card table. He crumpled to the ground, striking his head hard on the countertop as he fell.

Maddie reached the man just as he landed with a dull thud. Patrons around the restaurant rose to their feet to find the source of the commotion and gasped noticeably when they did. Maddie dropped to her knees beside the unconscious man and anxiously checked for a pulse. Finding none, she began the process of checking his airway and performing CPR. Her father reached the men in the booth just as the sweating man tipped over in his seat. The man with the welts watched on wide-eyed as Anthony cleared the area and began performing CPR on the second unconscious man.

Janet proved herself to be more than just a smiling order taker, as she hollered, "I'm calling an ambulance," over the growing racket.

Two men from another booth slid to a halt next to Maddie as she thrust on the coughing man's chest, explaining that they were CPR certified and could help with chest compressions. She turned the entire task over to them and joined her father to assist with the sweating man. It wasn't easy work in the cramped quarters, but leaning over the back of the adjacent booth allowed her access to help perform compressions.

After several tense moments, the sound of sirens began to fill the café as an ambulance roared to a stop just outside. Two EMTs quickly entered the building and began working on the coughing man first. Maddie and her father had regained a pulse on their patient, and he was breathing on his own, albeit with significant effort. He still appeared to be unconscious, but it was improvement.

They sat back to rest for a moment, just as two fire fighters burst through the doors of the diner. Their entrance brought them to their feet to make room for the professionals. As they stood watching, Maddie looked over at her father. Even in the cold air-conditioned restaurant, he was breathing hard and beads of sweat lined his forehead. In his prime, he could have run twenty miles and still had enough lung capacity to perform CPR for an hour. She still thought of him that way, like a daughter always wants to remember her father; strong, unbreakable, invincible, indestructible.

She was happy he was enjoying his retirement; it was well-deserved, but she hated that he was getting old.

Shouts from the paramedics working on the coughing man snapped her back from her thoughts in time to see them rubbing the defibrillator pads together. The man's back arched as the current tore through his torso, but still his breathing did not return. Again electricity surged through his body, again it tensed with energy, but the result was the same.

After several minutes, the EMTs gave each other a look and rocked back on their knees in defeat. An audible gasp from the back of the building cut through the silence. Someone else offered up a quiet prayer that Maddie could just hear over her right shoulder. She closed her eyes and turned her head away. She'd seen a lot of death already today, and it was barely lunch time.

The sweating man had finally stabilized and regained consciousness, and the fire fighters were talking quietly to him in the corner of the booth. They were encouraging him to let the ambulance take him to the hospital, and from the sounds of it, he wasn't putting up much of a fight. His dead friend on the floor offered the only incentive he needed at the moment. Even with the loss of one life, the room erupted with clapping as he was hauled to his feet and walked to the ambulance, mostly under his own power.

The third man had begun sweating as well, and he followed close behind. The welts on his face and arms were massive and covered almost every square inch of exposed skin. They must have been terribly painful, but they didn't seem to be the man's primary concern at the moment. His face had lost most of its color as well, and Maddie was hopeful they wouldn't lose another of the trio. He made it to the ambulance without incident and the EMTs clamored in and sped off after being assured by Maddie that she would handle the immediate situation inside the diner.

As soon as they left, she was on the phone with her office. It picked up after a single ring.

"Brody," she said without waiting for him to answer. "Close up the office and get down to the Diner. I have a deceased male, mid-40s. I need you to come down here and take care of this."

"What's going on?"

"Just get down here!" she said, her tone surprising even herself.

"I'll be right there, Boss," he said quickly before the phone went dead.

Maddie put her phone back in her pocket and looked at her father who was eyeing her thoughtfully.

"What are you thinking?" he asked.

"When I got to the station this morning," she started, "Frank was heading up to the lake to investigate a bunch of dead fish."

Her father nodded and she knew he was caught up. "Two might be a coincidence..." he said trailing off without finishing the sentence.

"But I don't believe in coincidences," she answered quickly. "I have to get back to the lake."

III

Even though it meant back-tracking a little, Maddie headed south out of the diner parking lot and straight for the bypass. Brody had arrived surprisingly soon after her call, and she was in no mood to waste any more time. Her father, having little to do the rest of the afternoon, had volunteered to ride with her. Two sets of eyes were better than one, he had reasoned. She didn't disagree.

"Have you ever seen anything like this, Dad?" she asked out loud as she drove. "Someone poisoning the lake water? Something polluting the air in that area?"

"I couldn't even begin to guess," he replied shaking his head. "If that land or water has somehow become poisonous, that would be a start, but it still doesn't totally explain Marvin's death."

Maddie hated to admit it, but she was thinking the same thing. The circumstances surrounding the deaths didn't seem to have many similarities apart from the proximity to the lake. And there was no indication that the elderly couple had even come in contact with the lake water.

"You know," her father offered, "this is probably a job for the EPA."

Maddie only nodded. She wanted a chance to look for herself. If she didn't find anything, she'd call in the big guns. They fell into silence as they drove; the lush, green undergrowth silently saluting them as they passed.

When they arrived at the lake, they both exited the vehicle and stood in momentary silence, surveying the landscape. The sun had arched high in the sky, beating down from overhead and continuing its relentless assault on their comfort. The light glimmered and sparkled off the lake as the inadequate breeze lightly danced across the water, rippling the surface. Even with her sunglasses on, the radiance was uncomfortable. Her father was clearly feeling the same effects, as his brow furrowed in a squint.

"Shall we?" he said finally, motioning toward the water.

While they hadn't spoken about it, they were both of the opinion that the clues to whatever was going on would be found near the lake, and not in the house. Maddie looked around as they walked, taking inventory of her current surroundings. John and Billy were long gone, and with them the bodies of her friends. The home appeared to be shut up tight.

They climbed the small ridge lining the shoreline and headed straight for the footbridge where Roda had been found. As they reached it, Maddie lowered her head to reduce the glare from the water. The narrow bridge spanned a man-made channel that fed a winding stream into the small lake, which eventually turned back into the same stream. In actuality, the lake was no more than a wider area of the creek, but the locals had decided to call it a lake, so there it was. The concrete walls of the inlet sloped gradually into the lake, allowing the water to flow freely over the spillway.

Maddie's eyes followed the flowing water and watched as it churned lightly at the base of the spillway. As her father stepped onto the bridge, she walked the shoreline looking for anything that might seem out of place. Nothing did. The air was fresh and clean, as it always was. She knelt by the lake and dipped her hand into the water. It was clear and cold, just like always. She sighed deeply. What had she expected to find? A pipe with green ooze spilling into the lake marked by a large sign and flashing neon lights?

Then something caught her eye.

Something sparkled in the water, just beneath the spillway. Something golden and bright, that didn't belong in a lake deep in the hills. She shifted her head to get a better look, but it disappeared. Her father noticed her antics and stopped his search to watch her.

"You got something?" he asked curiously.

"I thought I saw something, but now I don't see it anymore." As she finished the words, she rose back to her feet. Another brilliant flash of gold crossed her vision and again she bobbed her head to get a better view. There was definitely something there. She just had to get a good bead on it.

"They don't pull much gold out of this river anymore, do they?" she asked sarcastically.

"Not to my knowledge," Anthony replied. "Did you find some? My retirement fund could use a boost," he finished jokingly.

In the late 1800's the land in the Black Hills had been an abundant source of gold, causing thousands of optimistic pioneers to flood the area with shovels, pick-axes, and dynamite. Over a hundred years later, it continued to produce the rare metal in considerable amounts, enticing fun-seeking tourists to spend thousands of dollars every year for the chance to pan for it in the many rivers and streams that dotted the area. No one other than professional miners ever found any in significant amounts, but that didn't stop them from trying. And there certainly wasn't a large stockpile of it at the base of the Mitchell Lake spillway.

Anthony stopped joking as he watched her peel off her over-shirt and belt, and discard her sunglasses and badge on the ground beside her. She stepped tentatively into the lake, flinching and tensing as the cold water began to creep up her legs and thighs. By the time she reached the middle of the spillway, the water was almost up to her waist. She bobbed and nodded her head, searching continuously for the reflections that had caught her attention on the shore. Finally confident she had located the general area of the source of the light, she squatted down and immersed her arm almost to her shoulder.

Anthony watched uneasily as she rooted around for several moments in the water. Even though the current spilling into the lake was a gentle flow, he could see its force tugging on her body, seeking to pull her downward. He stood on alert, ready to dive in and pull her out, should she lose her balance and go under.

After several moments, her eyes widened and she pulled hard upward. Her hands emerged from the roiling waters clutching a large, round, golden object that shimmered brightly in the intense, overhead sun. She stood firm, looking first at the object and then up to the spot where she had found Roda's body; directly above where she was now standing. Finally she turned and started toward her father. He raised his hand above his eyes to shield them from the sun as he watched her wade back to shore wearing an inquisitive and perplexed look.

"What is it?" Anthony asked as she stepped onto solid ground and brought it closer to her face to examine it more closely.

She held a large, golden bowl, and while the metal shined brightly in the midday sun, the markings and design indicated it was anything but new. Symbols and etchings covered the entire outer shell. Lions chased ships between crashing waves, and in between the raised markings, hieroglyphs and primitive text twisted in, out, and around the more pronounced objects. The inside edge of the bowl was lined with twelve rudimentary markings in a circular pattern that gave Anthony the distinct impression of a clock. Maddie held it up at shoulder height so she could more closely examine it in the ample light. The metal shimmered intensely as she shifted it back and forth, sending dancing across their faces with every movement.

"I have no idea," she answered, cocking her head to the side and twisting it slowly. "If it was the Johnsons', they must have just gotten it. I've never seen it before."

"Do you think that's real gold?" he asked skeptically.

This time it was Maddie's turn to joke. "Should I bite it?" she said, moving her mouth to the edge as if to test the metal with her teeth. They both chuckled as she took another long look at it. "Have you ever seen anything like this?"

Anthony's only reply was a head shake. He tore his gaze away from the bowl and looked back out over the lake. "Should we put it in the truck and keep looking?"

"What if we don't have to?" she replied quietly.

Anthony looked at her with surprise. "You don't think this has something to do with what happened, do you?"

She ran a thoughtful thumb over one of the worn hieroglyphs and then turned to look at her father. "I can't explain it, Dad, but I do. It's right below the spot where I found Roda. And look at these markings. This thing looks ancient."

"Or a really convincing knock off," Anthony rebutted, pointing at one of the edges. "Look at how shiny it is. It can't really be that old. Besides, what are you implying? That because it looks old, it holds some magic ability to poison lake water and kill people in their la-z-boys?"

"What if it's lead?"

"Then it would have taken much longer to poison a lake full of fish and two full-grown adults."

"What if it's something else?" she said with dogged determination.

Anthony squinted at her as she held the object aloft. The thought struck them at the same time, as Maddie eyed the bowl and then quickly set it down in the grass. She wiped her hands absently on her shirt as if to wipe away any possibility of being poisoned by a foreign object. When she realized the foolishness of her actions, she marched quickly to her truck and retrieved the hand sanitizer she kept stashed in the door. Anthony watched her quietly, shaking his head and chuckling as she returned.

"What?" she said sarcastically as she laughed at herself under her breath. "I'm not taking any chances." She swiped away a clump of hair from her forehead that had freed itself from her ponytail, and as she did so, sweat trickled down the side of her face. Her dip in the lake had soaked her clothes and had provided incredible relief from the heat, but the effect was wearing off quickly.

Her father was still staring at her skeptically, but he had learned long ago to trust his daughter's instincts. She had a knack for being right in strange situations, so he wasn't going to put up a serious fight on this issue.

"So, you want to get it back to the station to get a better look at it?" he said finally.

"Yeah. I'll get Brody to do some digging online and see if he can turn anything up, and I'll have Billy come back out here and post some signs that the lake might be dangerous. I'll call the mayor and see if they can issue some kind of statement to the residents to stay out of the water for now." She finished with one last glance at the lake before turning back to her father.

"Tell you what," Anthony said. "I have to run a couple errands and one of them takes me right past city hall, so I'll stop in and deliver the message. I wanted to talk to him about his little rezoning proposal anyway." He finished with a wink and a mischievous smile that made Maddie shake her head.

For the past few months, her father had been entangled in a small dispute with the city over the property lines surrounding his small acreage east of town. The city had recently produced documents claiming that it actually owned one acre of his land; an acre, as luck would have it, that they wanted to rezone to expand their visitor information center. The city had offered to purchase the land at market price, but he was putting up a fight. In all actuality, he was more than willing to sell the property, but the market price they were offering was well below what he, and most of the locals agreed the land was actually worth. Of course, they had every right to claim eminent domain, but he wanted to put up just a big enough stink to get them to increase their offer a little.

"Can you deliver my message first?" she asked jokingly. "Before you tick him off?"

He grinned. "If you give me a ride back into town, I'll do my best."

Maddie shot him a playful look and then turned and headed back toward the truck. Anthony looked down at the bowl and then back up at Maddie's retreating form.

"Aren't you forgetting something?" he said as he leaned down to pick it up.

"Just leave it there," she called quickly over her shoulder, more loudly than she intended. "I'm getting a rag to wrap it in, just in case."

He stopped in mid-crouch and slowly stood back up while she returned with a large rag from the back of her truck. He watched her wrap the bowl carefully, shaking his head and chuckling the whole time. When she was done, she held it up for display, and nodded approvingly at her own work. She grabbed her belongings she'd discarded on the beach and carried everything back to the vehicle. She placed her golden treasure gently behind her seat on the floor of the extended cab before grabbing the hand sanitizer and meticulously lathering her hands again.

They drove quickly back into town, with Maddie shooting quick glances over her shoulder to ensure her cargo was undisturbed. She made a quick call to Billy to have him come up to the lake and post signs, and then another to Brody to check on his progress at the diner. He was just finishing up and said he'd meet her at the station to help look into the object she was bringing in. She dropped the phone roughly on the center console as she ended the second of the two very abrupt conversations.

The air conditioning on her wet uniform sent shivers up her back, and she felt herself actually longing for the heat of the outdoors. When they pulled up to the station, her father retrieved the package from the back and handed it to her. It was still shrouded in the rag she had wrapped it in, so she tucked it under her arm, gave her father a quick hug, and headed inside. She flipped her hand in a small wave as she stepped into the building.

The cool, inside air sent another quiver down her skin, but she didn't want to take the time to go home and change yet again. She'd be dry soon enough, and if they started digging into this thing right away, she'd be too preoccupied to notice how cold she was. Brody was already seated at the front desk and stood up as she walked in with her discovery. He looked at her skeptically when he saw the dirty rag bound up under her arm.

"What's in there?" he asked apprehensively.

"That's what we're going to find out."

IV

Maddie set the covered bowl on the table in the conference room and slowly unwrapped it. Even in the dimmer, interior lighting the object sparkled unnaturally. Brody stood in the doorway watching interestedly as she removed the item from its makeshift protective covering.

"Can you get some latex gloves from the cabinet?" she asked him.

"For that?" he said dumbly.

She turned and looked at him, raising an eyebrow as if to remind him who was in charge.

"Ok," he said raising his hands defensively. He walked out of the room and returned a moment later with a box of gloves in tow. He dropped them on the counter with a loud thud and leaned in toward the golden basin.

"This thing looks old and new," he said absently. "Look at those markings. They definitely look like some old, foreign text." He stopped talking and furrowed his brow. "Middle East origins, maybe?" he muttered finally.

"Have you seen anything like it before?" she asked hopefully.

"The text or the bowl?" he confirmed.

"Either."

"Not exactly," he said. "I saw all kinds of different languages on my tour, but nothing exactly like this. The markings on the outside look like some of the artwork over there, but nothing unique."

"Well, do you think we can find out what it is?"

"I'll scan them and upload them to the web." He shrugged as if trying to portray how easy the process would be for him. "If it's a language, it shouldn't take long to figure out which one. If it's just symbols, at least we should be able to find out about where and when it came from." He turned to head toward his computer and then stopped short and spun on his heels. "Why are we interested in this again?"

"I can't explain it, but I think this has something to do with all the death up at the lake," Maddie said as she stared absently at the shining metal. It was easy to get lost in the brilliance of the object. Finally she pulled her attention away. "Was Billy here when you got here?"

"Yeah," he called as he retreated down the hall. "He was just headed back to the lake to post those signs you wanted." His voice stopped for a second before continuing. "He said something about getting mileage pay for the day."

Was Brody trying to make a joke? Maddie thought to herself. Maybe Billy's enthusiasm and attitude were finally rubbing off on him.

Silence followed for a moment as she waited for him to return. Finally he appeared in the doorway with a scanner in his hands and began searching the walls for somewhere to plug it in. Finding the power he needed, he approached the bowl and reached to scan the symbols. Maddie grabbed the box of gloves and shoved it into his chest, stopping him in his tracks.

"Not without these," she said sternly.

He rolled his eyes slightly, but put the scanner down and complied with her request. Once garbed with the gloves, he flipped the bowl over and ran the scanner around the entire length of the outside. He checked the settings and scanned it again before confirming his satisfaction with the results and retreating from the room again.

Once he left, she snapped several pictures, then sat back and gazed again at the object, lost in thought. Finally she stood up and made her way back to her office. She had a friend who was a professor at the engineering school in Rapid City and she wanted to send him the pictures. She didn't know if he'd have any idea, but she didn't know of any other place to start. If he didn't know what it was, maybe he'd know someone who knew. At least it was something for her to do while Brody worked his magic.

She fired off the email with seven pictures attached and started the process of waiting for a reply. Paperwork from the diner incident was calling her name, so she pulled up the necessary forms and started on her second round of reporting for the day.

Early afternoon wore slowly on into late afternoon. Billy had long since returned, saying his shift was over and that he'd be back in the morning. She was just finishing her second round of administrative work and listening to her stomach rebuke her for skipping lunch, when Brody rounded the corner, waving papers high in his hand.

"Got some information," he said more excited than she had ever seen him. Apparently, he really liked this kind of thing.

"You know I hate to wait," she countered quickly.

"All the small markings that weave in and out of the objects are Babylonian hieroglyphs. I haven't been able to make out what they say though, because they're so worn."

When he started talking, she was leaning back in her chair. At the mention of 'Babylonian' she sat noticeably forward. She didn't know much about the Babylonians, but she knew they were old.

"What would it take to decipher the text?" she asked quickly.

He rubbed his chin discouragingly. "Well, there's the catch," he said slowly. "It was pretty easy to classify the symbols, but I can't get a good enough image of all of them to actually translate it. I need a computer with a little more processing power than what we have."

"And where might we find such a computer?"

He snorted loudly. "The city library," he said sarcastically, mocking the recent budget cuts and the quality of the equipment they left the department with.

She raised her eyebrows and nodded in agreement and looked away from the papers he was still holding aloft, turning her gaze to his face. It wasn't until then that she noticed he was sweating profusely.

"Brody, are you feeling ok?" she said, flashbacks from the diner flooding her mind.

He patted his stomach a couple times for effect. "Nothing a little Pepto-Bismol can't fix," he said sheepishly.

She eyed him hesitantly as he looked back over the sheets of paper. Suddenly, her computer chimed, indicating she had new email. She turned to her monitor to find a reply from the professor. She skimmed the email quickly, his message confirming what Brody had already discovered. He hadn't known anything about the object, but he had solicited help from the archaeology department and they had provided what they could.

"What does it say?" he asked, leaning in and craning his neck to see. She shot him a quick look and he backed respectfully out of her personal space.

"Same thing you already knew," she replied as she noted the highlights by counting on her fingers. "Babylonian...confirmed by the text and images...lions used often in Babylonian art...estimates it's dated between 600 and 300 BC...how the heck do they tell that from a few pictures?" she asked absently. She continued skimming until she reached the bottom. She read the last line, furrowed her brow, and then read it again.

"What?" Brody asked excitedly.

"He says they noticed some markings on the front leg of one of the lions that appeared to be text of some kind, but he couldn't be sure. They want a closer look." She stopped reading and looked up across the desk at Brody. Instantly, they were both moving in the direction of the conference room, Brody in front with Maddie close on his heels.

"Gloves!" Maddie said loudly as Brody swooped in to more closely examine the artifact. He groaned deeply and stopped mid-lunge to turn and slip the gloves into place.

"You didn't see what happened to those fishermen at the diner," she said firmly. "If this thing is the cause, trust me, you don't want any of that action."

Gloves in place, the pair flipped the bowl over and began to examine the legs of each of the lions in turn. By the third figure, Brody hollered.

"Got it!" he cried loudly jabbing his finger down on the face of one of the stamped lions.

She leaned in and he removed his finger to reveal small etchings in the front leg that were clearly designed to look like hair from the lion's mane. Upon closer examination, it appeared that it could be writing of some kind.

"How in the heck did he see that?" she asked absently.

Brody didn't answer. After removing his finger, he had moved back to allow her a closer look. She turned to look at him. His skin had gone completely pale and it was clear he was having problems focusing. He began to waver on his feet while he clutched his stomach. She grabbed both of his arms and spun him in the direction of the door. As she did so, he vomited forcefully and stumbled, catching himself against the wall at the last moment.

She cursed loudly and threw his arm over her shoulder and half-dragged him out of the room and down the hall to the first of the two small holding cells. As they reached the in cot in the first cell, he wheeled around and dropped hard to the bed. He lay there contracting uncontrollably as his stomach evacuated itself via his mouth. After several long moments, the spasms slowed and he rested; breathing hard, holding his abdomen, and groaning.

Maddie grabbed a wash cloth from the bathroom, rinsed it with cold water, and brought it to him and dabbed it on his forehead. His eyelids fluttered as his eyes threatened to roll back in his head while he rested. Maddie snapped her fingers above his face several times.

"Stay here!" she shouted at him demandingly. "Stay with me!"

She brought her phone quickly to her head and began calling for an ambulance. She punched one number before Brody's hand came up to stop her.

"I'll be ok," he said. "No ambulance."

"Are you sure?" she asked, eyeing him skeptically. "This is the same thing that happened at the diner, and one of those guys died! This is no time to be a tough guy!"

"I know," he said, still panting hard. "I feel better already though."

"You need to rest."

He nodded, still breathing harder than he should. "I think I just need to get home and sleep."

"You're not going anywhere until I know you're stable," Maddie said. "It's not up for discussion."

Brody nodded again.

"I'll call Billy and see if he can come and get you in a little bit."

Brody just nodded and rolled his head toward the wall. The rugged Marine was probably embarrassed that his boss was seeing him in that condition. But after three deaths and two other illnesses that morning, Maddie wasn't about to pass judgment on the toughness of her deputy.

She called Billy, bringing him up to speed. He offered to come right over, but she insisted he take his time. She wanted to be sure Brody was ok before she sent him home without any supervision. While she waited, she busied herself with cleaning up the mess. When the floor was cleaned, she stood at the edge of the cell, monitoring her patient. His breathing had slowed and become rhythmic, indicating that he'd finally fallen asleep.

She left him unattended and wandered back down the hall to where they'd left the basin in the conference room. She stood in the door, watching it intently... apprehensively. She looked down at her hands, remembering fishing it out of the lake bare-handed. She'd had more contact with it than anyone it would seem, yet she felt completely fine. Maybe this was all in her head. The thought of this thing actually causing sickness and death seemed preposterous. But after seeing

Brody reduced to little more than a weakened toddler, she was becoming more and more convinced.

Her thoughts got the best of her and she hurried down the hall to the bathroom and washed her hands thoroughly under the hottest water she could stand. In the middle of washing, a new thought struck her. She hadn't been paying attention to Brody all that closely. Maybe he had spent more time with the object than she thought. She quickly finished drying her hands and exited the bathroom just as Billy stepped in through the front door.

"Howdy boss," he said with a smile. The kid was too cheerful for his own good. It was no wonder he and Frank got along so well. "So, can I see this thing?" he asked as he raised his eyebrows with excitement.

She held up her hands to try and calm him down a little. "You can look, but I don't want you getting anywhere near it. I'm not putting your life in danger too."

He raised his eyebrows again and smiled, then headed down the hall. She followed close behind to make sure he did as she had instructed. When they got to the conference room, he stepped in slowly and stopped a couple feet short of the table. He looked intently at the bowl, peering closely at the markings on the side.

"You know what it says yet?"

"We're still working on it. We found what appears to be hidden text on one of the lions," she said pointing at the animal in question, "but we don't know what the language even is yet. We'll probably need to get an expert down from Rapid City, but I'm hesitant to let anyone get too close for now. I'm going to keep it here tonight, but I think I need to get someone here as soon as possible for some more thorough testing."

Billy squinted as he continued to study it. He opened his mouth and then slowly shut it again. Finally, he spit out his thought. "If this thing's toxic or something, don't you think someone would be looking for it?"

She rolled the thought around in her brain considering the ramifications, and decided that her young deputy was probably right. If the golden item in her office had anything to do with the deaths she'd witnessed today, it would certainly be an object that someone might be searching for.

"Why don't you get Brody home," she said finally. "I'm going to put this in a little more secure place and I'll probably spend the night here."

"You sure you should be hanging around this thing?" Billy said, concern lining his voice.

"I think you're right. Someone might be looking for it. I don't want to leave it alone." She looked at him and noticed he was staring hard at her, his brow furrowed. "I'll be ok," she reassured him, patting him on the back and guiding him down the hall toward the cell that Brody was sleeping in.

They shook Brody awake, and a surprised look crossed his face as he rolled over and saw Billy standing over him. He was looking better, but he was drenched in sweat that had soaked the cheap mattress he was lying on. This cell was occasionally used for cooling off drunkards, so the fabric had seen its share of sweat stains. At least this time it wasn't oozing with alcohol.

"Brody," Maddie started slowly, "how are you feeling?"

He closed his eyes as if to squeeze away cobwebs, but nodded affirmatively.

"I have another question," she continued.

He nodded again.

"Did you spend any time down in the conference room with that bowl this afternoon when you were researching it?"

A small hesitation before a third, sheepish nod. "I wore the gloves though," he reassured her.

She shook her head and patted him on the shoulder. "Billy's going to take you home. Are you sure you're ok to be alone or do you want to go to the clinic?" It was almost 5 o'clock, and the clinic would be closing any minute, but Maddie knew they'd stay open if she called and said she was sending someone over.

Finally, Brody croaked a response. "I'll be ok by myself."

"Ok, but keep your phone close. If anything changes, you call me. Got it?" She looked at him resolutely. He knew she wasn't playing around. He nodded one last time, before sitting up and letting Billy haul him to his feet.

"I'll call you when he's tucked in," Billy said with a smile.

"Thanks, Billy," she replied, patting him on the shoulder again. "See you in the morning," she said as they pushed their way out the front door and into the early evening sunlight.

She listened as Billy made an inaudible comment and laughed loudly at his own joke, presumably at Brody's expense. As the door swung shut, her desk phone began to ring. She hurried around the front desk and walked quickly to her office.

"Sherriff's office, Maddie Turner," she said bringing the receiver to her ear.

"Maddie," came the voice at the other end, "I'm glad you're still there. This is John. I've got the preliminary autopsy reports on Marvin and Roda."

At their names, Maddie's breath caught in her throat. She'd been so busy that she'd completely forgotten about the autopsy. She stood there in silence just long enough to get John's attention.

"Maddie?" he said questioningly. "Are you still there?"

"Yeah…yeah, I'm here," she said dumbly. "Sorry, it's been a long day."

"It might be about to get longer," he replied quickly. "Are you sitting down?"

V

"What can you tell me?" she asked hopefully.

"I can't find any cause of death whatsoever." He sounded exasperated.

Maddie had begun pacing her small office, but stopped in mid-step at his response. "What do you mean?" she questioned slowly.

"I mean, there's no logical reason that these people should be dead. There's no sign of a heart attack or stroke, or any other kind of sudden trauma that would cause life to cease. It's as if their hearts just quit beating and everything just..." he searched for the words "...turned off."

Maddie's blood was running cold as he spoke, and it felt like she was only hearing every other word. "There are absolutely no signs of struggle; no bruising, burn marks or scratches. There's no reason they should be dead."

"You said that already," Maddie countered, feeling frustrated, helpless and more than a little annoyed. She could hear the frustration in John's voice though, and she instantly felt bad for jumping on him like that.

"Sorry, Maddie," John offered weakly. "I just don't know what to tell you." He paused and silence hung in the air for several moments. "Does that help in any way?"

"It doesn't get me any closer to answers," she said wearily, "but it seems to make sense." Then a thought struck her. "Did you pick up a deceased fisherman from the diner this afternoon?"

"Yeah, he's here too. I noticed you were at the scene. Do you think they're connected somehow?"

"I know they are," she replied quietly. From her vantage point in her office, she could just make out the glimmering corner of the object she'd retrieved sitting on the edge of the table down the hall. She eyed it angrily. "I just have to figure out how. Is there anything that would make you believe the Johnsons and the fisherman died in a similar fashion?"

The line was silent for a moment. "Without looking into it further, I would say no. I mean, you were there, right? He was coughing and fighting for air before he passed out?"

"Yeah, he was definitely coughing."

"Then that would seem to me a different cause. If he was coughing like that, there should be some damage, however miniscule, to his respiratory system that would give us some indication to the cause of his death."

Maddie sighed deeply. That wasn't exactly what she wanted to hear, but it didn't really surprise her either. She'd suspected as much. She watched the man die, after all.

"Was there anything else on the preliminary report?" she asked hopefully.

"Sorry Maddie, that's all I have for now. If anything else turns up, I'll let you know."

She sighed again, thanked John for his hard work, and hung up the phone. She walked back out of her office and stood in front of the door, staring absently out the windows. Even in the summer, evening came a little earlier in the hills. Thousands of years of shifting and molding had made the tall rock walls exceedingly efficient at blocking out the sun. Long shadows were already tracing along the highway that ran in front of the sheriff's office as she watched a deer lope lazily across the blacktop.

Don't drink the water, she thought to herself absently as she watched the animal startle and then bound into the trees. She looked for the source of the deer's anxiousness to see a white SUV approaching from the west. It slowed noticeably as it passed the station, but then again, most vehicles did. She turned away from the door and walked back to the conference room and her mysterious treasure.

The rag that she had wrapped it in still lay on the table in a ball. She unfurled it and laid it over the top, covering the gold from sight. She didn't want to look at it anymore. Flipping the light off, she returned to her office and sat down hard in her chair. As she did, she heard the front door clink open.

She craned her neck to see who had just walked in, and not recognizing the man, looked toward the parking lot. Parked in front of the building was a white SUV. She stood up and walked out into the entryway to find not one, but three strangers standing at the front desk. All three wore black clothing from head to toe. The man in front wore only pants and a t-shirt. Deep wrinkles lined his mouth and eyes, revealing his age, but the well-defined muscles stretching his shirt sleeves seemed to test that theory. The men behind him, she noticed, were clad with long, black coats; unusual for the heat they were experiencing this time of year. All three had dark complexions and short, jet black hair that was cut in a manner reminiscent of the military.

"I'm sorry gentlemen, the office isn't really open right now," she said slowly, eyeing the three men with uncertainty. "But is there something I can help you with?"

The two men with the jackets didn't acknowledge her, but instead concerned themselves with scanning the interior of the office. She was getting a very uneasy feeling. The man in front looked her in the eye and addressed her question.

"It sounds like you've had an interesting day, Sheriff," he said quietly. His accent was thick, but she couldn't place it.

"And what would you know about it?" she asked pointedly. The men in back were annoying her and she was ready to put an end to their nosiness.

"The wonders of technology," he replied shrugging. "Years ago, it took days or weeks to hear about such oddities. Today, an hour after a school of fish washes up on a beach, it's all over Facebook and Youtube." He looked absently around the office and ran a finger along the paperweight that sat on the front desk. "Even in the middle of nowhere," he finished, returning his gaze back to Maddie.

"It's been a strange day," she confirmed. "Is there something I can help you with?" On a normal day, she didn't like repeating herself, and today was anything but normal.

"Where is it?" the stranger asked quietly, his face void of any emotion.

"Where is what?" she returned. Her years of keeping a straight face were serving her well. Despite the screaming in her head to ensure the golden basin's safety, she did not even flinch in that direction. She didn't want to tip her hand.

"Sheriff," the stranger replied quietly, "naivety doesn't suit you, and lying doesn't suit me. Now, where is it?"

"You're going to have to be more clear," she said, her tone betraying her annoyance with the questions.

"The item you pulled from the lake."

Instinctively, her hand moved to the pistol still strapped to her belt. In response, the man held up his hands, palms open and outward.

"There's no need for that," he said calmly. "At least not yet."

"I'm asking you to leave," she said resolutely. "I won't ask again."

"There are many items in this world," the stranger countered, ignoring her, "capable of killing two old people and a lake full of fish. We're looking for one in particular, and we believe you have it in your possession. We're not leaving without it."

She returned his steely gaze without flinching. "Unless you have a badge that says FBI, CIA, DHS, or some other 3-letter combination that outranks mine, you're not going anywhere with anything from this office."

The stranger glanced at the men on either side of him and tilted his head slightly. The side of his mouth flinched involuntarily as his eyes flicked back to Maddie's and then to the gun at her side.

"You're going to need that now, sheriff," he said quietly.

Slivers of light slashed through the office as Maddie and the two men drew their weapons simultaneously. Two barrels were leveled at Maddie's chest as she targeted the forehead of the gunman on her left. They stood motionless for several tense seconds while everyone contemplated their next move. While their weapons were intimidating, Maddie was still wearing her vest. If the shooting started, she was taking as many of them with her as she could.

"OK," she said as the familiar feeling of adrenaline began to flood her veins and cloud her thoughts. She held up one empty hand, palm outward, while keeping her gun leveled at the man's head. "OK, just hang on. I can't get it for you right now anyway," she lied.

"Why not?" the man replied. His demeanor never wavered.

"With everything that happened today, I wanted it locked down." She slumped her shoulders in feigned defeat. She just needed more time. "I put it in the bank vault and it can't be opened again until tomorrow morning."

The stranger flexed his jaw and eyed her with disbelief. His gaze shifted to the weapon in her hand and then to the men at either side of him. Clearly, he was looking to avoid a firefight if it was possible, but he was trying to decide if she was telling the truth and contemplating his superior firepower. After several more tense moments he squinted slightly and then tipped his head again at the two men, who lowered their weapons and returned them to their holsters. Maddie did not move hers.

"We will be back at eight tomorrow morning to accompany you to the bank. Please do not do anything foolish, Sheriff Turner. There's no reason anyone else needs to get hurt."

They turned quickly and walked back out the front door. Maddie watched down the barrel of her pistol as the back of the man's head disappeared from view. Only when the door clicked shut did she lower her weapon. She raced to the front door and spun the lock, listening for the reassuring click as it slid into place.

She watched them closely as they clambered back into their vehicle and slowly pulled out of the driveway.

The man she had spoken to returned her gaze as the car spun out of sight. Re-holstering her own weapon, she sprinted back to her office and grabbed her phone, dialing her boss's cell phone number in Rapid City.

"Hello?" he said nonchalantly.

"Mike!" Maddie said quickly. She was almost screaming. "This is Maddie. I need someone up here right away!"

"Whoa, whoa, whoa," he said, trying to catch up. "Just slow down. What's going on?"

As quickly as she could, she relayed the events of the day, ending with the three men who had just left her building. She peered out the front door to find the parking lot still empty except for her truck, but she wasn't convinced they weren't still out there…watching.

"These guys were really creepy, Mike. They meant business. I'll call Billy back in, but I need a couple more deputies up here as soon as you can send them."

"I'll call it in right away," he said reassuringly. "For the time being, keep the door locked and your head down."

"Thanks, Mike," she said, slowly lowering the phone back to its base.

A loud pounding at the front door forced a small scream to escape her lips and she turned back toward the door. Slowly, she raised her head to see who it was. Relief washed over her as she recognized the face of her father cupping his hands around his eyes and trying to peer through the glass.

She ran to the door, unlocking it quickly and pulling him into the building.

"What's the rush?" he said jokingly as she yanked on his arm. Once in the office, he turned and looked at her face for the first time. It was white as a sheet. "What's going on? Is everything ok?"

She dropped her head and a tear streaked down her cheek. Embarrassment at her weakness washed over her and she felt the need to apologize.

"Sorry," she offered feebly, wiping the tear away.

Her father just hugged her. "Tell me what's going on."

For the second time in ten minutes, she relayed the recent events, filling her father in on all that had happened since he left that afternoon. Her father watched her closely as she described the encounter with the three strangers. Strangely, when she finished, he was smiling.

"Honey, I can't even tell you how proud I am of you. Staring down the business end of any firearm is no laughing matter. That took amazing courage."

She stood there sniffling. "And now I'm crying like a baby."

Her father laughed. "That's just the adrenaline wearing off," he said running a hand lightly over her shoulders. "It's got to come out somewhere," he said smiling. "Sometimes people wet their pants."

"Nuh uh," she said giggling.

"True story," he replied. "I've seen Marines soil themselves like 2-year-olds," he said laughing.

She giggled harder and gave her father a hug. He squeezed her tight, then broke away and turned to lock the door before glancing out the window.

"What are you doing?" she asked, knowing the answer before she even finished the question.

"If you think I'm letting you stay here by yourself with those guys out there, you're crazy. Even in a hurry, it'll take the deputies from Rapid City almost half an hour to get here. If those guys decide you're lying, it won't take them that long to get in here and get what they want." He glanced out the window again, and content there was no activity, turned and walked back toward her office. "Where do you keep your extra guns?"

She followed him to the back and retrieved her key to the weapons cage. Opening the cage, she handed him a shotgun and a box of shells, which he promptly loaded into the weapon.

"Where is the bowl now?"

"Still in the conference room," she replied nodding down the hall.

They headed in that direction and she sat down at the table while Anthony remained standing, leaning up against the door jamb. He rested the shotgun over his shoulder and stared at the covered bowl thoughtfully.

"At least you know there's something to this thing," he said motioning to the cloth covering. "That guy said it had the power to kill, right?"

Maddie nodded her head and shrugged her shoulders. "Maybe he was just saying that though. That's a lot of gold. It would be worth killing for."

He let the idea sink in, nodding in agreement. Silence fell between them as they each lost themselves in their own thoughts. All they could do now was wait for the cavalry to arrive.

Maddie's mind drifted back to the handkerchief she'd found in Roda's hand. Had Roda witnessed Marvin's death and killed herself intentionally? Or had she carried the bowl to the lake with the hanky, trying to throw it in, and touched it accidentally? She feared she would never know the truth, but decided resolutely that no matter how bad it was, her friend would not have deliberately taken her own life. She had to believe that.

Finally, Anthony raised his head and looked at his daughter, causing her to snap back into the moment. "I'm very proud of you, Maddie," he said quietly. She looked up at him, a surprised look on her face. She knew he was proud of her, but she wasn't expecting to hear it again at this moment.

"Your instincts were right on. You thought quickly on your feet and you knew exactly what to do to guard what was under your protection." He smiled at her slowly. "You would have made a good FBI agent."

She chuckled and looked back down at the table. She opened her mouth to speak, but never got the chance. Without warning, a brilliant light flashed from the front of the building, rocking the structure and sending shards of glass into their short hallway. Time slowed down as she watched her father spin away from the eruption and crouch behind the wall he'd just been leaning against. Even in the back of the building, she could feel the heat from the explosion that had peeled the front of the station open like a sardine can.

Inaudible shouting resonated from the front of the building, mixing with the shouts of her father, motioning frantically in her direction. It was only then that she realized she was still seated at the table. Time caught up with her and she dove to the floor under the table, removing her weapon from her holster and cursing at her slow reactions.

She twisted her head to peek just above the table at the front door. Three dark-clad figures entered the building and began fanning out in a small sweeping pattern. She looked back at her father who made eye contact and nodded slightly. The dark-clad strangers had decided not to wait until morning after all.

VI

Maddie's ears were ringing as she crouched under the table. Her father was kneeling behind the wall only three feet away, but the open door between them prevented her from crossing the distance to be closer. He peeked around the doorway and then turned to her, motioning wildly with his hands. She held up her hands questioningly and shook her head to advise him that she didn't understand his hand signals. She wished desperately that she'd taken more interest in his work when she was younger.

Exasperated, he stopped motioning and pointed his finger like a gun, pointed to her, and then pointed out the door. She nodded her understanding. Then he held up a hand indicating he wanted her to wait. She nodded again. Smoke and dust were beginning to filter into the room, making visibility out into the entryway limited, but she could still make out shapes when she dared to sneak a peek.

Anthony surveyed their situation, quickly realizing they were going to need some help. They were in a room with no viable exit, and the three strangers were closing in quickly. It was only a matter of time before they found them, and the more distance between them when that happened, the better their odds would be.

He reached up and grabbed the cloth that was covering the golden bowl. He listened for a moment as footsteps moved through the entryway, crunching on debris as they progressed through the building. Grasping the cloth tightly, he pulled hard, causing the object to topple loudly to the floor right in front of Maddie. She jumped back in surprise as the item clamored to a stop on the floor.

The noise worked. The footsteps from all three men stopped as they focused their attention in the direction of the commotion. Anthony kicked the bowl hard, sending it skittering loudly out of the conference room toward the men. Then he pointed at Maddie.

Two of the men made the mistake that Anthony was betting on. As the bowl slid out into the lobby, their eyes followed it, giving the trapped duo the opening they needed. Leaning around the door, Anthony fired his shotgun straight into the chest of the nearest man, dropping him like a rock. From her position under the table, Maddie fired two shots toward the only figure she could see through the haze. She knew her shot was wide, but hoped it would be enough to slow him down. She watched his body wheel to her right as her bullet tore through the flesh of his upper arm. He let out a yelp and jumped to his left, out of firing range.

Only the man in the center maintained his view of the conference room, and returned several short bursts of fire in their general direction. It was apparent he expected them to be standing, as the bullets whizzed over their heads and tore through the back wall.

Maddie and her father dove back behind the cover of the walls and table, and crouched down as the two remaining assailants sent several rounds of return fire toward their makeshift bunker. Anthony gave Maddie a quick thumbs up, confirming they had just evened the odds a little in their favor. They could hear shouts in a foreign language between the bursts, but could not make out anything that was being said.

Without warning, the shooting stopped.

Anthony looked at Maddie and wrinkled his brow questioningly. As he peeked around the corner of the door, his eyes widened and he spun back quickly. His head spinning back into the room was followed closely by a grenade that had been lobbed in their direction. It landed on the floor with a hard thud and skidded to a stop at the back wall. Maddie rolled to her right and curled into a ball, bracing for impact. Anthony kicked the edge of the table hard, tipping it over on its side between them and the grenade.

The force of the explosion drove the table into their collective bodies, knocking them both hard against the wall. Maddie felt the weight of the table crush her chest, forcing all the air from her lungs. She gasped hard at the debris-filled air, feeling a sharp pain on her left side that most certainly indicated a broken rib or two. Finally finding her breath, she coughed hard and clutched her side.

Through the ringing in her ears, she could just make out the sound of approaching voices and tried to push the table off of her. It didn't budge. Through the effort, she noticed the throbbing in the back of her head, and reached her free hand back only to withdraw two bloody fingers from behind her skull. Stars danced through her vision and she blinked hard to rid herself of them. Through the fogginess, she looked over at her father. A small trace of blood trickled from his lips and had dripped onto the collar of his shirt. She stared at him dumbly, pleading for him to answer her. His eyes were still open, fixed on a point beyond the exterior wall, but he did not answer.

Suddenly, the table lurched and shook as it was removed violently from her body. Her ribs actually hurt worse with the pressure removed. A dark figure entered her line of sight and stood over her menacingly. Her head had begun spinning and she felt very strongly that she had to vomit.

The figure relayed foreign instructions to the other man, who disappeared down the hall, retrieving the bowl and then handing it to the first man. He knelt down in front of her and tipped his head, examining her closely. His mouth began to move, but Maddie couldn't make out any words. Slowly the fog began to lift and the language began to make sense.

"...asked you not to do anything foolish, Sheriff," the man was finishing. "Now we have been forced to spill more blood." The man looked back and forth between his fallen comrade and Anthony. He pursed his lips before muttering something unintelligible and placing the golden basin next to Maddie's face.

"Please forgive me," he said as he touched the cold metal to her cheek.

She stared at him helplessly as he pressed the edge into the soft skin on her face. He squinted at her as she watched him, then shifted his grip on the bowl and pressed harder. The cold metal bit into her neck as he cocked his head and furrowed his brow before removing the object from her face and leaning back. Slowly, he rose to his feet and turned to the other man, handing him the bowl. Without warning, he twisted back toward Maddie, his fist arcing to the side of her chin. She felt the force of his knuckles on her face before everything went dark.

******

Maddie found herself standing in a large field of wild grass in a wide valley. Hills covered with brown, dead evergreen trees rose impossibly high on either side. At the far end of the valley was a small lake. She walked toward the lake and noticed something floating near the beach. As she got closer, horror gripped her as she realized it was a body. She started running, but her feet wouldn't carry her the remaining distance. She tried running faster, but no matter how hard she ran, she just couldn't cross the gap. Just as she was about to give up, the space between her and the lake closed dramatically and she found herself standing on the shore, her toes immersed in the icy water.

Her hand shook as she reached for the body that bobbed gently in the small waves. Slowly, she rolled the body over in the water to reveal the pale face of her father staring absently back up at her. She tried to let out a scream, but the sound wouldn't come. Suddenly, her father looked directly into her eyes and smiled.

"Wake up, Maddie," he said cheerfully.

She took a step back at the words and tripped on the bank, landing hard on the ground. A tear streamed down her cheek.

"Wake up, Maddie," he repeated, louder this time.

She shook her head fearfully.

"Wake up!!" he screamed.

She blinked hard, and when she opened her eyes the space in front had been voided and only darkness remained. In her ear, a steady beeping called to her and she tried to turn her head to find the source of the noise. Fleeting fear gripped her again when she realized she couldn't turn her head and she tried to blink it away.

When she opened her eyes for the second time, she was staring at an acoustical ceiling. The grid in the ceiling tiles came in and out of focus as her eyesight slowly adjusted to the dim lighting. She sat up slowly, wincing at the pain in her ribs and wanting to vomit from the spinning in her head.

"Slow down boss," said a quiet voice beside her. "You took some nasty hits. You might want to take your time." She looked around her to see the face of Billy Murphy smiling back at her. His hand was resting on her shoulder, trying to keep her from moving too quickly. "I'm glad you're ok," he finished.

"Where am I?" she said absently.

"We're at the clinic. If you hadn't woken up soon, they were going to move you to the hospital in Rapid. They were concerned you had a brain injury."

Maddie reached up and touched the back of her head, remembering the collision from earlier that had caused her initial wooziness. The wound had been wrapped in gauze, but even through the fabric, she could feel a sizeable lump. The memories were starting to come back to her. She saw her father's face…and blood trickling down his lip onto his collar.

"Where's my father?" she asked suddenly.

Billy's face fell at the question. "Um…" he stuttered. "I'm sorry boss. He didn't make it. You guys were in a nasty mess. The station's got a hole blown in it big enough to drive your truck through. I don't know how you walked out of there…"

He was still talking, but Maddie wasn't listening. Tears streamed down her face as she forever etched the last image of her father into her memory. Her throat burned with the tears, but she didn't fight them. She'd lost so much today, but this last loss threatened to break her. She sobbed openly causing Billy to stop talking abruptly.

"Can I get you anything?" he asked quietly. She nodded her head and waved him off. The kid was young, but even he had some tact. "I'll be outside if you need me," he finished before exiting the room.

Maddie lay back in the bed and cried for what seemed like hours. She curled up into a ball and cried herself back to sleep.

When she awoke for the second time, the only source of light in the room was the sliver that crept in under the door. She stared at it absently for a moment before slowly rising to her feet and taking a few tentative steps toward the door. She turned on the light and winced in pain as her eyes revolted against the assault.

She stepped out into the hall to find Billy and a nurse absently flipping through channels on the TV. They both stood as she appeared around the corner. Her head was still pounding, causing slight dizziness, and her ribs ached painfully, but she badly wanted to leave. Since she wasn't technically in a hospital, she hoped they wouldn't fight her on it.

"Billy, can you give me a ride home?" she asked quietly.

He looked at the nurse questioningly who was trying to shake her head at Billy without Maddie noticing.

"Do you think that's a good idea right now?" Billy asked her in reply. She looked at both of them resolutely, and Billy knew it was pointless to argue further. "I'll take you to your house," he said, "but I'm going to be checking up on you regularly."

"Fine," she replied as she headed toward the door. "What time is it?" she asked as they exited the building and crossed the parking lot. In her condition, it was slow going, but the more she walked, the better she was feeling.

"Just after two," Billy said, checking his watch and rubbing his eyes. "You were out the first time for almost four hours."

By the time they reached the car, Maddie was already feeling much better.

Fresh air must be good for concussions, she mused inwardly.

They drove slowly through the quiet town, watching as a handful of leftover bikers wandered the empty streets in search of one last party for the night. She lowered her head and closed her eyes, but all she saw were the faces of her father and friends.

"How did I get to the clinic?" she asked, trying to tear her mind away from the sadness.

"The deputies that Mike sent up from Rapid hauled you out of that mess and brought you over here." He looked at her with concern. "You're lucky to be alive. We thought we'd lost you."

"Where are they now?"

"They all went back to the station."

"All?" she questioned.

"A sheriff's station was attacked," Billy said excitedly. "When the deputies called Mike, he sent an army up here. There's camera crews crawling all over that place!"

She mulled it over silently. "How is it that none of them were at the clinic trying to get pictures of the one survivor?" She wasn't asking for any attention. Far from it. But one would think people would want to hear what she had to say since she was there.

Billy gave her a quick smirk. "Mike may or may not have implied that you had been moved to the hospital already." His face fell a little. "He knew you'd need a little privacy after today."

She leaned her head back on the headrest taking in the information. It wasn't helping her head.

As they pulled into her drive, Maddie was surprised to see her truck in front of her garage. She pointed a thumb in its direction and raised her eyebrows at Billy.

"Deputies brought that over too," he said with a shoulder shrug. "Didn't have a scratch. Keys are in the ignition. Don't get any dumb ideas though," he finished with a smile.

He dropped the car into park and started getting out to help her into the house. She waved him off.

"I can make it myself," she said resolutely. "The walking feels good."

Billy watched her intently as she and made her way to her front door. He rolled his window down as she crossed in front of the vehicle.

"The nurse said you should get checked out in Rapid as soon as possible," he called to her. "You probably have a concussion. You're supposed to rest until then."

"You're not supposed to boss me around," she responded with a smile. "Thanks for the ride. If you're not busy tomorrow, I may leach a ride into town too."

"No problem, boss," he said. His voice sounded relieved that she wasn't going to try and drive herself to the hospital. "See you tomorrow."

"Good night," she replied as she slipped the key into the lock and gave it a turn.

The lock clicked loudly and she swung the door open into the entryway. She exhaled slowly as she shut the door behind her and leaned against it momentarily. It felt good to be home.

She made her way slowly down the hall and dropped the keys on the counter as she passed the kitchen. Reaching for the living room light switch, she suddenly stopped in mid-motion. Seated in the chair facing the front door was a dark figure watching her every move. Her blood ran cold in her veins as a now-familiar accent pierced the night air.

"Welcome home, Sheriff Turner. I hope you aren't too badly injured."

VII

Maddie flipped on the light forcefully and turned to face her intruder. Her head was still pounding, but the adrenaline that was starting to flow was taking the edge off. She didn't care what he was doing here. She was going to kill him, or be killed in the process.

She still held her belt in her hand, and when she noticed he was not holding a weapon, she drew her pistol. Dropping her belt, she strode across the floor and placed the barrel of the pistol directly in his face. He did not flinch. Her blood was boiling and the hatred she currently felt threatened to send her over the edge. She curled her lip at him, looking as menacing as she could manage in the moment.

"What are you doing here?" she hissed.

The man was holding one hand up, palm outward and open. Clearly he wasn't here to kill her or he'd have done it when she walked into the dark room. She was still contemplating shooting him. She would have no problem claiming self-defense, given the situation.

"Please do not shoot, Sheriff," the man said. His words were pleading, but his manner appeared to be anything but begging. His voice didn't waver a bit.

"And why not?" she asked pointedly.

"I am sorry for the loss of your father," he started slowly. "Believe me when I say I did not want it to come to that."

"I don't believe you. And that doesn't change the outcome," she retorted, pushing the gun into the skin under his chin.

"If you are to kill me, my soul is prepared," he said calmly. "But I have undertaken a journey that I would like to see to the end."

"So did my father," she spat at him. "Give me one good reason why I shouldn't pull the trigger." She was tired of his voice and wanted to see her father's murderer pay.

"If you kill me, you will never know the truth about who you are."

She squinted at him and took a small step back. He could be stalling, but then again, he had entered her home unarmed, and had not killed her even though he had ample opportunity to do so. Was it possible this stranger knew something of her biological parents that even her father hadn't told her?

"You've got about three seconds to tell me what you know," she replied coldly. "If I don't like what I hear, I'm putting a bullet in your head and going to bed."

"I know that your last name isn't Turner. It's Knox. I know that even though your mother died a criminal, she started as a guardian of the truth. And I know why you survived today while everyone around you perished." He watched her reaction closely as his words sunk in.

Maddie lowered her weapon slowly. The stranger watched as the barrel gradually dropped toward the floor. She eyed him carefully and for the first time noticed that his clothes were bloodied and torn, and a trace of crimson was trickling from his right leg onto the carpet. His left arm rested gingerly on his stomach, as blood from his upper bicep had started seeping through a rag he had tied tightly around his shoulder. He did not have those injuries when he left the station.

"What happened to you?" she said eyeing him suspiciously.

"Shortly after we left your office, we were attacked." He continued to watch her reaction closely. "All of my men are dead, and I was lucky to escape with my life."

A pang of satisfaction ran through her bones. "Couldn't happen to a nicer fella," she said out loud. The man squinted in sorrow at the words. Her thoughts drifted to her own deputies and for a moment she felt remorse for her words. Her father raised her better. The least she could do was honor him in death. She lowered her head and looked at the floor. "I'm sorry," she offered weakly.

The man breathed heavily. "Thank you," he said curtly. "I am also deeply sorry for what we have taken from you. Our mission is not one to end lives on this soil. Until now, America has been our great ally, and we do not wish to hurt her people." He hung his head in shame. "I hope in time that I can earn your forgiveness."

Forgiveness? In time? Her mind was screaming at her. How long did he think this relationship was going to last?

"What are you talking about?" she finally spit out at him.

He breathed deeply and winced, presumably from the pain inflicted by his wounds. She felt a small measure of satisfaction at his discomfort, considering the aches she was currently feeling because of him and his men.

"The item you found in the lake was most definitely responsible for the death and illness you witnessed today."

She wanted to interrupt and ask her own questions, but at least he was starting to make some sense. She hoped he'd get there eventually. He stared hard at the floor searching for his next words.

"Twenty six hundred years ago," he began again slowly, "my people were attacked, and our city was razed to the ground. Everything was destroyed, and anyone that survived was taken into captivity to live as slaves. In addition to losing our freedom, children, and homes, we also lost a very valuable object; one that possessed the power of Yahweh."

"Yahweh?"

"Our God has many names. That is but one."

"So that thing was given to your people by your god?" she asked snidely. "For what? To kill other people?" She didn't bother hiding her disbelief. "Why didn't you use it when you were attacked?" she finished sarcastically under her breath.

"Not OUR God," he corrected. "The Living God."

"God?" She said incredulously. "As in Jesus Christ, crosses, Israelites? That God?"

The man nodded.

Maddie considered herself to be an educated person, but she had to admit her Jewish history was a little rusty. She didn't recall any golden bowl that possessed the power of God though.

"You better start making sense," she said menacingly as she raised the gun back toward his head. Her ribs reprimanded her with the movement, but she pushed the pain back stubbornly.

"When our city was attacked," he continued, "we sought a way to protect the Ark of the Testimony, but even our best plans were flawed."

"Wait, wait," Maddie said, holding up a hand and eyeing him thoughtfully. "Did you say 'Ark'?"

He nodded.

"Are you talking about the Ark of the Covenant?" she asked, her eyebrows drooping with sudden disinterest.

He nodded again.

"I've heard the bedtime stories," she said with a snort.

"War? Disease? Famine? Death?" the stranger interjected. "These are not bedtime stories, Sheriff. They are nightmares."

"Well, I've seen Indiana Jones," she rebutted sarcastically. "That thing in the lake wasn't the Ark of the Covenant. It's a bowl. Let's try a different story. One that ends with you in prison…or an asylum."

"What you know about the Ark is only half of the truth, Miss Turner," he replied.

His manners were starting to get on her nerves. "Well, why don't you cut to the chase and tell me the other half then," she said, adjusting her grip on her pistol and leveling it clearly at his head.

He did not waver. "For centuries, the world has searched for the Ark. Its location has become somewhat of a legend, as you know by your movies." His dark eyes twinkled in the dim light, like small chunks of glowing coal in the bottom of a fire pit. "Our city was under siege for over two years. When it was evident we would not survive, our priests gave us a command from God that broke the will of every Hebrew man, woman and child. We were to melt down the Ark of the Covenant; the living manifestation of God among His people." He paused, laboring under the pain of his words and the hole in his shoulder. "It meant that God was no longer with us." He paused again, collecting his thoughts. "When it was done, the priests recast it into seven unique items to be hidden in the courts of King

Nebuchadnezzar, the king who had conquered us. When the time was right, we planned to recast it and restore our covenant with the Lord. We never got the chance."

He bowed his head and whispered something inaudible under his breath.

"Why not?" Maddie questioned when he lifted his head again. Despite her anger, she found herself becoming interested in the story.

"A small group of Babylonians discovered what we had done. We had appointed a protector to watch over the items in Nebuchadnezzar's courts, but the Babylonians scattered them across the earth and almost killed our protector. Only his favor with the king and our God saved him. We have been searching for them ever since." When he finished, he lowered his head a second time and whispered inaudibly again.

"So, in twenty-six hundred years of searching," Maddie began, "how many have you found?"

The man didn't look up from the floor. "Only three. The item you had was the fourth."

She stared hard at the top of his head. This was all just a little too incredible to believe.

"Ok," she said, testing him. "What were the raised figures on the bowl?"

"Lions and ships," he replied without hesitation. "The inside was cast to represent a sundial."

"Why?" she asked quickly.

"Those items were consistent with Babylonian symbols. We felt it would be easier to hide them in Babylon if they looked Babylonian."

"And what was written on the lion's leg?"

He paused and Maddie thought she saw him flinch slightly at the question. She felt a surge of satisfaction at finally catching him a little off guard. He hadn't expected her to find that in the few hours she possessed it.

"The script on the bowl reads 'Who has kept us alive'. It was one line of an ancient Hebrew prayer," he replied quietly. "All seven objects were marked similarly. The text simultaneously identifies the objects and marks the order in which they need to be melted back down."

She chewed over his last comments carefully. "Why is it killing everyone?" she asked finally.

"Our people have battled many enemies over the centuries. During our struggle with the Philistines, the Ark was captured and taken back to their country." He still had not raised his face to look at her. She thought she heard shame in his voice. "They were afflicted with all manner of disease, plagues, and death. So much so, that they finally returned the Ark to our people. When the Ark is possessed by someone who is not a child of Israel, they suffer the same fate. Even in its current form, it possesses the power of God, and belongs only to His people." He paused for a moment, but this time she didn't speak. After a brief silence, he continued. "When our people left Egypt and traveled to the Promised Land, the tribe of Levi was appointed to care for the Ark of the Covenant. Only members from the tribe of Levi are allowed to touch it and care for it. All others perish."

Maddie was stunned at his last words. "But I..." she began.

Suddenly, he raised his head and looked her in the eye. "When I touched it to your face and you didn't die, I knew there was only one explanation. Before we were attacked, I was able to get some answers." He was speaking more quickly now. "Your mother did not begin her life as a criminal. She was once one of us. We trained her. She was part of our family. She was assigned to America, but greed and the pursuit of power twisted and warped her beliefs. She was excommunicated, but that didn't make her any less of a

Levite. The blood that flowed in Levi's veins...in our ancestors' veins and in your mother's...flows in yours."

She shook her head disbelievingly at him and took a step back, but somehow deep down, she knew it was the truth. Everyone else that had come in contact with the item was either dead or very sick. She'd held it in her hand and had felt no effects.

"You belong with us," the stranger said meeting her gaze again, "and I could desperately use your help."

She eyed him angrily and her heart was once again filled with rage. "You murdered my father! You brought death and disease to my town! You tried to kill me! And now you want my help??" The request was preposterous and her voice didn't betray her aggravation. "I'm still considering shooting you," she finished with a hiss. Her voice was shrill and her breathing was ragged. Her head still pounded, but it was nothing compared to the pounding in her enraged heart. The hand holding the gun shook almost uncontrollably as it hovered over the man's head.

"I can understand your anger with this situation and me personally. I can only beg your forgiveness and pray that in time you can come to forgive me. We truly did not want to harm you. Knowing the truth only makes my transgression that much more severe." He paused for a moment. "The Ark is not a harbinger of death. Once restored, it will reunite our people, bring balance back to our land, and help put a stop to the endless line of bloodshed in that region. Its importance to our people cannot be understated."

"Stop saying 'our people'," she spat at him. "You are not my people."

His head was bowed again and for the first time she realized he was actually praying in the midst of their conversation.

"What are you praying about?" she asked absently.

"For the words to convince you to assist me."

"Why do you need my help so badly?" she asked. "Don't you have a group of thugs waiting in the wings that you can call up to help you get it back?"

He shook his head slowly. "They would be too late."

"Why?" she asked bluntly, not liking where this conversation was headed. "Who took it?"

"Your Department of Homeland Defense. And if we don't get it back tonight, they'll have it locked up so tight we'll never recover it."

Maddie shook her head and laughed sarcastically. "Now I know you're insane," she said finally. "Why do you think I would help you do anything, least of all attack members of the United States' Department of Homeland Security? This is my home. I may have descended from your people, but your problems are not my problems. That's not my fight."

"There's more you need to know," he finally answered quietly.

She didn't answer him, but continued burning holes in the top of his skull with her eyes.

"I knew your mother personally."

Her glare softened faintly at the mention of her mother.

"We were matched in training because of how well we worked together. But, that partnership developed into something more; something we should have never allowed." He stopped and took a deep breath. Maddie couldn't be sure, but he appeared to be crying. "For many years after arriving in America, your mother led a double life; a life that I…God help me…chose to ignore. Our superiors found out about it before I would admit it, and I was given orders to eliminate her." His voice was crackling, and now Maddie was sure he was fighting back tears. He bowed his head even lower. "I couldn't do it. When I confronted her, she admitted to everything." He stopped suddenly, and Maddie eyed him closely to make sure he was still conscious. He had lost a lot of blood. Tears streamed down his cheeks as he looked up into Maddie's eyes only for a moment. He blinked away the salt water and dropped his head back toward the floor.

"Admitted to what?" she asked finally.

He paused, searching for the words. Finally, he gave up the search and just blurted it out. "Killing the family of the man you called father."

A cold shiver ran up her spine and hatred instantly filled her heart once more. "That's a lie!" she screamed at him, bringing back her fist for a heavy blow. "My father would have told me!" Her ribs were pleading for mercy, but she kept her fist poised over the man's head as she snarled down at him. She wanted him to see it coming. He never looked up.

"You may strike me if you wish," he said remaining calm, "but that does not change the truth."

His words slowly sunk in and she dropped her hand to her side. Rage filled her, but this time it was not with the man in front of her. She spun away from him, and hurled her pistol across the room. She screamed with pain and anger, but felt a satisfying twinge as the weapon struck a picture, shattering wood and glass with an audible crunch. She dropped to her knees, buried her hands in her face and bawled. The stranger said nothing; only watched as her emotions poured from her eyes into her palms. With one last sniffle, she wiped her cheeks and looked back up at the man. Tears streamed down his face as his gaze met hers.

"There is one last thing," he said slowly. "Only a full-blooded Levite is endowed by God to care for, and therefore, possess the Ark." Time slowed down, and she watched as a tear broke free from his cheek and splashed onto his torn, bloodied shirt. His eyes betrayed the pain he was feeling, but it wasn't from the wounds that covered his body.

"On the night I confronted your mother, she begged for my forgiveness…"

"No…" Maddie objected, shaking her head and slowly sliding backward across the floor.

"…I took pity on her and believed her lies…"

"No…" she pleaded, fresh tears wetting her cheeks.

"We spent the night together one last time," he said, bowing his head again. "When I woke up the next morning, she was gone. I never saw her again. And I never knew until today that she carried my child in her womb when she fled."

"NO!" she screamed loudly as the sound of her voice pierced her own eardrums painfully. She rolled into a ball and buried her face in the shag carpet. Tears soaked the floor as she tried to wash away the unrelenting mercilessness of the day. She wished the ground would open and swallow her whole, but comfort would be a long time coming.

The seconds felt like hours as she lay there sobbing uncontrollably into her hands. Suddenly, she felt a soft hand on the back of her head. She stiffened at his touch, but did not stand up. The smell of gun powder and blood permeated her senses and she finally sat up into a sitting position. She did not bother to wipe away the tears this time.

She stared hard at the man, trying to decide if the act was genuine. He was crying as well. She'd already lost her father today, and she wanted desperately to not believe him, but a small voice in the back of her mind told her he was telling the truth. Her life had completely unraveled in the course of eighteen hours, and she wanted…needed…to believe there was a purpose for it. She was starting to fear that she would have to see this through, one way or another. She couldn't just walk away from it. She sniffled loudly and her breath caught in her throat like a child who had cried too hard for far too long.

"Where did they take it?" she finally spluttered.

The stranger was momentarily taken aback. His hand was outstretched to her, and it hung in midair as he regained his composure. She didn't know if he was expecting some kind of joyous reunion embrace, but it would happen over her dead body. As far as she was concerned, her father was dead because of the stranger in front of her. Eventually, they would have to square that between them.

"They have an office in Rapid City. I believe they have taken it there and will move it in the morning to a more secure location. They believe me to be dead," he continued, pointing to the rag on his shoulder and the blood trickling from his leg. "For the time being, they are not in a hurry. But we have to act quickly."

"I think you might be jumping the gun on the 'we' part," she replied matter-of-factly. "What you're asking me to do is insane. It violates everything my position stands for. I'm supposed to work with other agencies, not attack them! How can I even be sure you're telling me the truth?"

She spoke the words convincingly, but even she didn't believe them. She knew it was the truth, and in his eyes, he knew that she knew it was the truth. And she knew that too. All that was left was to decide if she wanted to see the truth to the end or if she wanted to cut her considerable losses and walk away. If her father had taught her anything, it was not to bite the hand that feeds you. But he also taught her not to back down from a fight and that bullies, more often than not, just needed a good punch to the nose. The part of the bully was currently being played quite successfully by the

Department of Homeland Defense. She slumped her shoulders and stared down at the floor.

"What exactly are you proposing?"

VIII

The moon had almost completed its nightly trek across the sky as dawn rapidly approached. Maddie stared absently at her reflection in her living room window and wondered how her life could have possibly come to this in the past 24 hours. Yesterday morning, she had woken excitedly to go see her friends who, as she now knew, somehow brought home the angel of death with them from their trip to Europe. Now she was preparing to help with a suicide mission against agents of her own country...adopted or not.

She reflected on the day's events while her beliefs and allegiances fought a grudge match over her mind and threatened to drive her mad. She knew in her heart...in her soul...that what the stranger told her was true. After another hour of talking, the man had finally introduced himself as Jacob Segal. He described thrilling adventures that spanned the globe only to result in failure or disappointment. He exuded undying faith and confidence even as he recounted fallen friends, lost allies, and countless dead ends. For all his stories, Maddie believed he had a long, lonely life of searching, heartache, frustration, and defeat, only to be made worse by the discovery that he had a daughter in her 30's that he never knew about.

She found it fascinating that a man could dedicate his entire life to the search of something that he would most likely never find. Only three of the seven pieces had been found in twenty-six hundred years. And yet, he had held his prize in his hands, only to be separated from it almost immediately. Even when he won, he lost. She almost felt pity for him even though his actions and words commanded the exact opposite. Maybe she had a nurturing, motherly side after all.

She turned her attention to him and watched intently in the window's reflection as he cinched up the wrapping around his shoulder and pulled on a clean t-shirt that she'd found in one of her closets. As he pulled it down over his abdomen, Maddie noticed countless marks and scars tracing his skin like a medieval crossword puzzle.

The pants she couldn't help with though, so his bloodied pair would have to suffice. He lifted the right pant leg gingerly and inspected the wound that had dotted her floor with crimson. Several small holes peppered the outer edge of his leg, but the bleeding had stopped. She knew from experience that pattern was made from a shotgun blast. Six inches to the right and he might have lost the entire foot. He added weight to it tentatively and took three small jab steps to his left, testing the leg with quick movements. Satisfied that it would do for now, he wrapped it in gauze and dropped the pant leg back into place. The BB's, much like the slug in his left arm, would have to be removed later.

"I am ready, Sheriff," he said finally as he reached behind his back, withdrew his pistol, and handed it to her.

"Maddie," she said correcting him. "I'm about to not be a sheriff any longer."

"Stick to the plan," he said reassuringly as he placed his hand on her shoulder. "It will protect you from discovery. Are you wearing your vest?"

She nodded, retrieved her own pistol from the floor, and handed it to him.

They climbed into Maddie's truck with her behind the wheel and slowly pointed the vehicle toward Rapid City. The sun had yet to light up the morning sky, but already birds could be heard chirping in the distance as they drove. Maddie soaked it up. She took Main Street one last time, hoping that she wasn't making the biggest mistake of her life, and saying good-bye to her home just in case she was. No matter the outcome, she didn't know if she could come back to this world anyway.

"The sun will be up soon," Jacob said. "We must hurry if we are to have any darkness to work with."

He was understandably in a hurry, but she realized some of it was due to concern for her. They could do this in broad daylight, but if she stood any chance of returning to her former life, they needed limited lighting.

"We'll be there in about 25 minutes," Maddie replied. "We'll have some cover."

Her mind was still racing as they made their way through downtown. She had so many questions she wanted to ask and so many answers that she couldn't put together on her own. She was still trying to form a question when he suddenly held a hand up by her face.

"Slow down," he said quietly as he stared hard between two buildings.

"What is it?" she asked, her adrenaline already starting to pump.

"Circle the block," he answered with a hiss, "but try not to look obvious."

Obvious would have been leaving the gauze wrapped around my head, she thought to herself sarcastically, but she did as he asked and circled up one block and then back down a side street. The maneuver brought them a little closer to the feet of the hills that lined the city limits. Jacob watched intently in between the houses until he got a clear view of his quarry.

"Yahweh is with us tonight," he said. "That's the van that attacked us. If those men are still in town, our job just got much easier." He bowed his head and spoke softly under his breath again. Maddie started to roll her eyes and thought better of it. A little divine help wouldn't hurt.

Maddie circled back toward Main Street and parked the truck down an alley just off a side street. The two exited the vehicle silently and quickly made their way back to the house where the van was parked. Jacob peeked around a garage to get a better view of the van and then turned back to Maddie.

"I need one of them out in the open," he instructed as he took out his gun and motioned for her to swap weapons back. As he took his gun back he retrieved a silencer and screwed it into place. "If it's one of our guys, I'll put a bullet in his brain. If it's not, we'll walk away."

Maddie nodded and rounded the corner of the garage and strode to the house. Two lights glowed in the windows, even at the early hour, indicating someone was at least awake. She scaled the steps quietly and knocked softly on the back door. She didn't want everyone inside to know she was there.

She stood there for a moment listening for any sounds from inside the house. Silence greeted her in return and she was almost ready to knock again when she saw a shadow cross in front of the curtains. She stood straight and put on her best concerned face as the door slid open a crack and the light on the porch above her came on. She squinted against the light and took a small step back.

"What do you want?" came a tired, gravelly voice from behind the door. It opened just a crack to reveal one eye staring back at her.

"Hi," Maddie said, doing her best to act nervous. She spoke rapidly, hoping to avoid any objections before she could get her story out. "I was just running with my dog and he got away from me. I think he ran through your yard. Have you seen him?"

"Nah," the man said as he started to shut the door in her face.

"Please," she begged as she gave him her best 'lost puppy dog' look that she had in her arsenal.

"Ah geez," the voice replied as a tall, well-built man opened the door and poked his head out into the light. Tattoos covered his right arm from his shoulder to his elbow and his long, dark hair was pulled back into a tight ponytail. He rubbed his eyes and continued his complaining. "Look lady, I've been in the…"

He never got to finish his whining as two crimson dots appeared on the right side of his temple and the same color painted the door behind him to his left. His eyes widened slightly as the life drained quietly from his face. He slowly began to tip forward and it dawned on her almost too late that she should catch the man and avoid a clamor. She threw her weight into him straining as his mass slowly overpowered her. It was just enough to slow him down and she slowly lowered him to the step with minimal noise.

She listened intently to see if they had been discovered. After several moments of silence, she decided they were in the clear. As she stood back up, she was joined on the step by Jacob.

"I take it this was our guy," she said sarcastically.

"That's why I shot him," he said matter-of-factly.

She squinted at him and cocked her head questioningly. "We're going to have to work on your sarcasm." she said quietly.

They swapped weapons back again, moved the body around the corner out of sight, and then entered through the back. Maddie was in the lead as they rounded the corner into the kitchen. It was completely empty.

Maddie held up three fingers and raised her eyebrows questioningly. Jacob nodded his answer, swung his finger in a circle indicating they should finish checking the first floor, and then pointed upstairs. She nodded her understanding. They completed their check of the first floor, but found nothing. As they rounded the corner into the living room, the stairs came into view and Jacob nodded toward them. Quiet, inaudible voices drifted down the steps toward them. There were definitely two distinct voices, and Maddie thought she heard a third.

They tiptoed to the steps and made their way painstakingly upward. The house was of considerable age and the stairs squeaked lightly with every step. It was only a matter of time before they hit the wrong step.

They found it half way up.

As Maddie stepped to the edge of a stair, a loud squeak resonated through the silence. Both of them closed their eyes and clenched their jaws with frustration. She moved her pistol behind her back as Jacob moved behind her. The voices that had been talking quietly stopped altogether.

"Chuck!" bellowed a voice from above them. "You got my omelet yet?"

The other two voices erupted in laughter as Maddie and Jacob looked at each other in relief. Clearly the men above them didn't think they were in any danger. Maddie shrugged her shoulders and continued up the stairs, with her new associate close behind. They reached the small landing at the top of the stairs and Maddie looked over her shoulder, nodding to Jacob. He nodded his head in return, and she took a deep breath and stepped into the light of the room.

Three men sat around a table deeply engrossed in a game of cards. On a table beside them, the golden bowl sat safely enclosed in a glass case. Maddie wasn't sure if they had done that or if Jacob's men had put it there when they took it from the sheriff's office. Either way, at least it wouldn't be hurting anyone like that.

All three men wore the identifiable dark pants and shirts of tactical gear and one of them still had his weapon strapped to his hip. The others had discarded their guns on the table next to the bowl and its glass case. Two of the men had their hair cut short, clearly flaunting a military affiliation. The third had long hair pulled back tight like the man downstairs. All of them were built like tanks.

The man with the gun noticed their presence first. He looked up just in time to see Jacob raise his weapon to Maddie's head as he stepped into the room behind her.

"Gentlemen," Jacob started slowly.

The man with the gun began reaching for it as the other two glanced at their discarded weapons, too far away to be of any help.

Jacob continued. "This is Sheriff Maddie Turner of the Hill City Sheriff's department. Hand over the item that you stole from me earlier tonight and I will let her go."

The three men exchanged glances before returning their gaze to the intruder with the gun. Maddie shifted her stance slightly, sliding her arm deftly to her side. All eyes remained on Jacob.

The man with the gun, clearly the man in charge, drew his weapon and leveled it toward their heads. "And what do I care if a sheriff of some dumpy little town dies?" he asked coldly, an evil smirk spreading across his mouth. "You're insane if you think you're walking out of here alive."

"I told you," Maddie said to Jacob, feigning arrogance as she shifted slightly one more time.

He yanked her roughly and put the gun right in her ear. "You'd let an American Citizen die?" he asked the man pointedly. "An officer of the law?"

"To keep you from getting this?" the man with the gun retorted. "Absolutely."

"Disappointing," Maddie said quietly as she shifted one last time. With the last movement, her hand was twisted to point directly at the man with the gun. The man with the long hair saw it first.

"Gun!" he roared as Maddie squeezed the trigger, sending two bullets into the chest of her adversary.

The other two men were in motion instantly. The long-haired man tipped over backward in his chair and rolled to the table where he had abandoned his gun. Jacob kicked the table they were using for cards as hard as he could, sending it into the other man's chest and knocking him backward. He rolled as he hit the floor, but his momentum put him almost under the table with the weapons.

Maddie split away from Jacob and fired another shot at the long-haired man, who had retrieved his gun and was preparing to return fire. She missed wide right. Jacob sprinted and dove at him, but his wounded leg did not allow him the power he was apparently used to. He hit the man in the midsection, preventing him from firing at Maddie, but the blow did little else. The man held his ground and hammered the butt of his pistol into Jacob's back, driving him into the ground with the force. Jacob made a sickening groan as he hit the floor, but it was enough to give Maddie her opening. She fired two more shots into the man's chest, dropping him in a heap on top of Jacob, who groaned again with the force of the dead weight.

The last man had seen his opening and used the opportunity to retrieve his weapon. He swung it back quickly and trained it on Maddie's chest. She twisted her pistol in his direction, but she was too late. Two shots pounded her chest, as she fired wildly in the man's direction. She dropped to the ground, fighting to regain the breath that had just been forced from her lungs. The pain in her chest was almost unbearable.

The last man looked over at Jacob's body, buried beneath his companion's massive form. Confident he was no longer a threat, he side-stepped the broken table and strode toward her menacingly. As he walked, he hefted his weapon and sneered at Maddie as she writhed on the floor, still struggling to breathe. The air was returning to her lungs, but pain seared through her chest with each gulp. Taking a straight shot to the chest at that range almost always broke a rib or two. Compounded with her earlier injuries, she was lucky to still be conscious. As the last man approached she got the sense that the pain would be short-lived.

Her gun lay on the floor just out of reach, and she rolled over to make a grab for it. The man laughed at her and kicked her hand out from under her, causing her to fall to the ground and grab her chest in pain. He picked up the gun and tossed it leisurely across the room, well out of reach. Her spirits died as the metal clanked to a stop in the corner.

He looked back at Jacob, ensuring he was still not a threat, and caught sight of the bowl sitting on the intact table. A wicked smile crossed his lips as he kicked Maddie sharply in the stomach and crossed the room. The impact almost made her vomit.

"You know what this bowl does, Sheriff?" he asked snidely.

She watched as he put on a pair of gloves and slowly removed it from its case. Then he turned back to her.

"They tell me this thing kills anything it touches," he continued. "I've never seen it, but I'd like to."

His wicked smile turned maniacal. She did her best to look defeated. It wasn't a difficult task.

As he crossed the room toward her again, he held the gold aloft, admiring its beauty as he walked.

"This thing's like thousands of years old," he said. "Amazing, huh? Lucky you. This will be the last thing you see on this planet. Sure hope you're going somewhere good."

He knelt down beside her as she squirmed back away from him. She took a swing at him, but he caught her wrist in mid-air and jerked it hard. She winced and let out a stifled scream at the movement.

Slowly, he brought the bowl up to her hand and she instinctively held up her open palm as if to defend herself. He sneered and pushed the gold to her hand. She blinked at it and then up at her attacker. His eyes squinted as he looked back and forth from her hand to her face, as if he was still waiting for something to happen.

"Well, what do you know," he said finally. "All this for a piece of junk that doesn't even work."

She smiled at him, causing him to squint questioningly.

"It works fine," she said as she put all her weight into her shoulders and shoved the gold into the man's face.

He let out a yelp as he caught his own reflection in the shiny metal rising to meet him, but the sound of his surprise died quickly with him. His grip on her wrist loosened as his lifeless body fell slowly backward to the floor. The bowl rolled free of his grasp and clattered to the ground beside him.

She sat breathing slowly for several moments until she was satisfied she could bear the pain in her ribs. She stood and crossed the room to where Jacob lay unconscious under the dead body of the long-haired man. Wailing in pain, she put her weight into the man's side, rolling him onto the floor and uncovering the man she hoped was still alive.

Placing her fingers under his chin, she tipped his head back and searched for a pulse. Finding one, she sat back against the wall, surprised at her own relief. She stared intently at his face, asking unspoken questions and waiting for his silent answers. She sat there for several more moments, catching her breath and taking stock of her own injuries.

Finally, she slapped Jacob hard on the chest, causing him to startle and open his eyes. He blinked hard before raising his head from the floor and looking in either direction.

"Did we win?" he asked quietly as he rubbed his chest where she slapped him. He tried to sit up, but groaned at the effort and laid back down.

Maddie shook her head at him with mock disdain before standing up and retrieving the bowl and his gun from the floor.

"So…" she started slowly, looking down at him and then back to the bowl. "What's next?"

He pulled himself to a sitting position and looked deeply into her eyes.

"I go back to Israel," he said, measuring his words. "You go back to your life." He held his hand out motioning for her to give him his weapon back. "Everyone was shot with my gun. Two shots to the chest should be enough to convince even the most determined investigator that you were a hostage who was left for dead."

She eyed him thoughtfully, contemplating her next words. She couldn't go back to her old job. Not after this.

"And what if I don't want to go back to my life?" she asked quietly. "There's nothing left for me here."

He cocked his head in surprise, reading between the lines. "I guess we would have a lot of catching up to do," he said slowly, turning away and staring at the floor.

She leaned into his field of vision just enough to get his attention. He turned back and looked at her, meeting her gaze.

"Let's start with breakfast," she said finally. "I know a great diner."

ABOUT THE AUTHORS

Robert Palmer resides in Sioux Falls, SD with his wife and two of his four amazing children. He is an avid golfer, writer, football fan, father, and husband.

Eva Palmer lives in Portland, OR with three of her five brothers. She enjoys spending time with her friends, playing basketball and soccer, and plans one day to attend the University of Oregon.

PALMER

Hostages

Robert A Palmer

Copyright © 2013 Robert A Palmer

Published by
Skowndral Hill Publishers
Sioux Falls, SD 57107

Originally published as *Hostage Desert*

First Edition: April 2013

Robertpalmerbooks.com

ISBN: 1484167384
ISBN-13: 978-1484167380

DEDICATION

To my wife and children;
My greatest inspirations.

CONTENTS

ACKNOWLEDGMENTS

I would like to extend my deepest, most sincere thanks
to my wife for encouraging me, supporting me, and
always believing in me.
Even when my stories don't interest her.

I

Jack Stanton stood listless on the edge of the highway, peering into the distance…searching. His heels hung off the edge of the pavement, and he could feel a large pebble from the gravel ditch pushing up through the sole of his left shoe. He'd been walking for hours though, and the effort to move his foot wasn't worth the gain. His shabby clothes hung loosely off his 6'1" frame in a manner that indicated recent weight loss. His blue eyes sparkled in the sun; eyes so brilliantly blue his wife used to joke that clownfish could mistake them for home.

A light breeze ruffled the edge of his un-tucked shirttail. He closed his eyes and raised his arms as the air rushed over him, cooling him and kissing the perspiration at his armpits and his chest. December in this area didn't normally produce a sweat, but the unusually warm weather was coaxing it out of him today.

He opened his eyes and a glint in the distance caught his attention. He turned to watch as the sparkle edged closer, the reflections of heat waves on the road distorting the oncoming vehicle.

Looks like a van, he thought. *Maybe this one.*

As the vehicle came fully into view, he raised his arm and put out a thumb. It was close enough now he could hear the sound of the tires on the road. The sound deepened as the vehicle began to slow. The squeal of the brakes, like nails on a chalkboard, confirmed it.

Music to a vagabond's ears, he thought, sighing deeply. He lowered his hand and leaned down to pick up the dusty pack by his feet.

The van lurched to a stop five feet in front of him. A man sat in the driver's seat, chewing on a toothpick and eyeing him suspiciously over a pair of small, but stylish sunglasses. He looked to be in his early thirties. Sweat stains lined his hat and t-shirt; proof that Jack wasn't the only one feeling the effects of the winter heat. The brunette in the passenger seat rolled down the window and smiled at him. Her hair was pulled back in a tight ponytail that presented a neat appearance. Jack thought it made her look rough and haggard. Her smile, while appearing genuine, looked like a shark smiling at its dinner. "Need a lift?" she said with a southern twang.

Jack eyed them both cynically for a moment, chewing on the inside of his cheek. Then, with his free hand, he reached around to the back of his pants, his fingers finding a familiar metal object tucked into his belt. His hand reappeared from behind his billowing shirt holding a large silver revolver. "Lady, you have no idea," he said slowly, as he trained the weapon at the brunette's forehead.

Her eyes squinted involuntarily as she stared down the barrel of his weapon. Slowly, her lips pursed and she looked down into her lap. The driver shuffled his gaze between her and Jack, but he never moved a muscle. Suddenly, the woman lifted her head back toward Jack, at the same time raising a double-barreled shotgun over the edge of the window, and pointing it straight at Jack's chest. The driver turned his attention solely to Jack. He sucked audibly on his toothpick and pointed an equally impressive pistol in Jack's direction. "We were counting on that, partner," he drawled with a lop-sided grin.

Jack chuckled sarcastically, slowly lowering the weapon to his waist before throwing it to the side. It landed with a hard thud in the gravel on the side of the road. He dropped his bag and raised both hands skyward, watching thoughtfully as dust billowed up from the duffle and floated away on the light breeze. The brunette exited the vehicle, leveling the shotgun at his chest as she did. When she got both feet on the ground it was her turn to reach behind her back and withdraw her hand with a metal object in tow. He knew they were handcuffs before she even tossed them at his feet. Even over the sound of the engine, the metal clinked loudly against the pavement as they landed.

He looked down at the restraints, and then back at the brunette out of the top of his eyes. She stood poised…waiting, still leveling the shotgun at his chest. He knelt down, picked up the handcuffs, and began attaching them to each wrist.

"Nuh uh," she said shaking her head mockingly. "Behind the back."

His lip curled as he looked up at her snidely, before he placed his hands behind his back and complied.

"Move," she said motioning to the back of the van with her gun.

He started walking. After two steps, he turned back and nodded to his gun. "Make sure you bring that with."

"Why's that?" she replied sarcastically.

"Cause I'm going to want it back."

The brunette chuckled, clicking her tongue at him, and followed him to the back doors. By now the driver had excited the vehicle and was standing at the back. He sneered at Jack as he rounded the corner, and wiped at

3

the sweat on his forehead with his hat. He put his hat back on and pulled open the double doors on the back of the vehicle. With only two small, tinted slots for light in the cargo area, the interior of the van was especially dark in contrast to the brilliant overhead sun. Jack's gaze followed the light that now sliced through the shadows, and revealed three other men, handcuffed and shrouded with black bags over their heads. All three men jerked involuntarily at the light's intrusion.

"What the?!?" Jack began.

His question was cut off in mid-sentence as a bag was forced over his head, and a foot met his lower back, forcing him violently into the van among the others. As he landed, his knee struck hard on the floor and something hard, possibly an elbow, dealt him a fierce blow across his jaw.

"Say a word, and we put a bullet in your head," the brunette said coldly while cackling loudly.

He laid groaning for several moments as the doors to the van were slammed closed, smelling the fetid, mustiness of the bag that now resided on his head. He listened to the muffled voices and footsteps of his captors as they returned to the front of the vehicle, slammed their respective doors, and pushed the vehicle into gear. Tires squealing, Jack's body was again pounded viciously as the van lurched forward with its new cargo.

If he thought it was hot outside, it was stifling in the cargo area. Within minutes a bead of sweat found its way down his back, sending a shiver up his spine. He flattened his back against the side of the van forcing his shirt to absorb the drop.

As the van rocked, he flexed his leg slowly, working out the tingling in his knee cap. As he worked it, he could feel the fabric from his pants pulling against his skin; a sure sign he'd split his knee open and his pant leg was now covered in blood. He sat up and wrenched his neck, trying to work the bag into a position that would allow him to inspect the wound. Even if he'd succeeded, the light in the cargo area probably would not have allowed much of an examination. Eventually he gave up and turned his attention to the other residents of the vehicle.

With the bag and dim lighting, he could barely make out shadows, but he could distinguish the three other forms, slumped against the walls. Two of the men lay on their sides, while the third sat upright, swaying slightly with the motion of the vehicle. Jack cleared his throat. None of them reacted to the noise. He cleared his throat again, longer and louder than the first time. Still no reaction.

He turned his head from side to side, straining to hear and trying to get his bearings. "Hey," he finally whispered to the other figures. He strained for a response. "Where you guys from?"

"Man," a whispered hiss returned, "shut up before you get us killed."

Suddenly, the van pitched as the brakes were applied forcefully, and all four men tumbled toward the front of the cargo bay. Curses harmonized with limbs on steel and squealing brakes, as the vehicle came to an abrupt stop. The front doors slammed, followed seconds later by the back doors opening and light pouring back into the van. The driver leapt into the cargo bay, grabbed one of the men by the handcuffs and began pulling hard. The man grunted and squealed loudly as he was hauled out backwards and viciously thrown to the ground.

Placing his pistol to the back of his neck, the driver whispered into the man's ear. "Do I need to make an example of you?"

Jack could hear the man pleading for his life, and he wondered inwardly if the man was soiling himself.

The man beside Jack began to stir. "I'm going to vomit," he said suddenly. "I get motion sickness."

"Then vomit," the brunette cackled in his direction.

The man rolled to his side and groaned. He was breathing hard, and Jack did his best to remove himself from the splash zone, should the man heave. The van already stunk of body odor. Bile didn't need to be added to the mix.

Outside the van, the driver eyed the back of the man's hooded head thoughtfully for a moment before placing the pistol back in his belt and dragging the man back to the van the same way he'd removed him. He kicked him in the side as he positioned himself back in the van, sending him sprawling into the other three men. "Another word," the driver said, "and next time I'll kill the first person I get my hands on. We can pull this job with three just as easily. More money for all of us that way."

Beneath his hood, Jack rolled his eyes. The two were doing what they felt necessary to display dominance, but he doubted seriously that they were in any real danger. Organized crime had rules, and one of those rules stated that handlers didn't go around whacking their own crew for no good reason. Especially before the job was even done. That kind of behavior didn't sit well with the bosses.

The brunette cackled again as the driver slammed the door hard, muffling the last half of her fiendish taunt. The men lay in a heap for several moments, the matter of the soiled pants settled as dampness crept into Jack's thigh. He squirmed away from the man lying next to him, cursing under his breath as he moved.

Slowly, the vehicle lurched forward again and Jack listened to the methodical humming of the tires on the well-paved road. Only a few minutes had passed before the man who had spoken earlier began gagging. Jack could feel the man's feet tap his as he lurched with every heave. The cargo bay was quickly filled with the smells of urine and partially-digested food. With the new smells added to the potpourri of body odor, Jack had to fight the urge to heave himself.

None of the passengers said another word for the duration of the trip as Jack turned his head from side to side alternating polluted breaths. After fifteen minutes, the van began to slow and made several abrupt stops and turns.

Must be in the city, he thought. He strained to hear any distinctive sounds, but apart from the sound of other vehicles, very little was audible through the steel shell of the vehicle.

After several minutes of stopping and turning, and another round of vomiting from the man at the back, the van finally came to a complete stop. The engine continued to run, but the vehicle rocked as both front doors were slammed shut. The back door was thrown open violently and light invaded the small space. Even behind the hood, Jack had to squint.

"Tubby," the driver said, tapping one of the men on the leg. "Get out."

The man brought his head up suddenly as if trying to look around. "Me?" he said hesitantly.

"No., the other fat man," he answered sarcastically, kicking out at the man viciously. "Yes you. Let's go."

The man shimmied his way to the back of the van, dropped his feet off the back, and stood up gingerly. The brunette tossed something soft at the man's feet as the driver stepped forward, and removed the hood and handcuffs.

"Go inside and put that on," the driver said. "Your instructions are in the front left pocket. When you're done, walk back out through this door."

As he spoke, he moved back to the doors and shoved them hard. Before the doors slammed shut, Jack was just able to make out a pile of red at the feet of the tubby man beneath his hood.

Seconds later, the van lurched forward again and turned a corner. Again the van came to a stop and the strange process was repeated, this time with the man who had soiled himself. On the third stop, it was Jack's turn.

"Chatty Cathy," the driver said, tugging on Jack's pant leg. "Out."

Jack slid to the back of the van and stood up, leaving the sick man in the van by himself. As the driver unhooked his handcuffs and removed his hood, the brunette tossed a blue pile at his feet. His eyes squinted against the unrelenting sun as he tried to focus on the object she'd dropped. He stood motionless, trying to gather his bearings, just long enough to get her attention.

"Don't make me repeat the instructions," she said tapping her hip to indicate the weapon hidden there.

Jack bent down and picked up the clothes lying at his feet. By the time he stood back up, the two were back in the van and pulling away. He was standing on pavement, and rows of cars lined a parking lot to his right. A group of teenage girls walked past and looked at him skeptically. One of them giggled, elbowed her friend, and tipped her head in his direction. He smiled at them curtly, before clutching the pile of clothes in his arms.

This team had been assembled for one purpose; a kidnapping. And now he stood at a side door of a mall, during the height of the holiday shopping season, with only a small piece of paper for instructions. Unless those instructions contained a little bit of magic, this figured to be a really short trip.

II

Jack looked back in the direction the van had left and headed toward the door. Inside, he unfolded a corner of the clothes he'd been given just enough to reveal a security guard uniform. He looked around cautiously, and then headed down a side corridor toward the nearest bathroom. The girls from the parking lot were just ahead of him, but they'd turned their attention away from him, and were now laughing loudly and striking poses like mannequins in front of a nearby department store. He smiled at them painfully...longingly.

Must be about sixteen, he thought to himself as he watched them give up on the mannequins and round the corner out of sight.

He snapped back to his task and entered a nearby bathroom, making his way directly to the back wall of the restroom to the handicap stall. There was no use changing in cramped quarters.

Once changed, Jack exited the stall and discarded his old clothes in the trash near the door. The clothes seemed to fit fine, but the shoes were about a size too small. He'd fix that at the earliest opportunity. He carefully removed two small silver items from the heels of his old shoes and tucked them safely near the top of his sock, before throwing the shoes into the trash with the rest of his clothes. He would circle back and retrieve them if time allowed. Reaching into the right breast pocket of the uniform, he found an envelope containing a small, typed note. He needed to study it only for a moment to memorize every detail. Since he was a child, Jack's memory had been almost photographic. He remembered everything almost instantly, which made him ideal for this type of situation.

After returning the note to his pocket he looked down at his watch, habitually readjusting the Velcro strap that held it in place. 2:47. According to the note, he had approximately eight minutes to get in place. He moved to the sink and splashed some cold water on his face to revive him a little. The putrid ride in had more of an impact on him than he thought.

He exited the bathroom and traversed the corridor into the mall, making his way leisurely to his ultimate destination. As he walked, he did his best to avoid eye contact, occasionally bringing the radio that he'd been provided to his ear as if listening to an important conversation. He could not afford being delayed by a patron needing assistance.

Once in place, Jack stood in a corner, conspicuously eyeing the appointed department store entrance. A brightly dressed Santa Claus made his way into Jack's line of sight, loudly 'ho ho ho'ing' and waiving to nearby children. The smells from the food court beckoned to him, and he eyed the sample trays ravenously. He hadn't had a real meal in several days, and the smells were almost intoxicating. Popcorn strings and candy canes hung loosely from a nearby Christmas tree and he wondered seriously if anyone would notice if he grabbed some for a snack.

Christmas music blared over the intercom, joyously welcoming patrons to open their checkbooks. There was a time when Jack loved the sounds of the holidays. Now it just brought back painful memories that cruelly twisted his stomach in a way that a lack of food or a nauseating van ride couldn't come close to matching. He sighed and returned his gaze to the store entrance.

Suddenly, the alarms at the store's entrance began to chime and a woman exiting the store looked around apprehensively. Her daughter raised her eyebrows and Jack could see her mouth to her mother, '*Mommy?*' She was a cute kid, sporting extremely sparkly jeans, a pink puppy dog hand bag, and a coat that was entirely too thick for their current weather. Her blonde hair was pulled back in two tight pigtails. She looked to be about five or six. Jack's stomach twisted again.

As he watched, a security guard approached the woman from behind and held out his hand as she began to frantically search her purse and the bag of items she had purchased inside. The little girl had gone from curiosity to apathy and was now pushing on her mother's pant leg, and she was putting her back into it. The mother tugged back impatiently on her leg as she gestured wildly at the security guard.

As the two adults engaged one another, Jack noticed the jovial Santa slowly meander toward the unfolding scene. He was waiving to the daughter, who had moved behind her mother's legs and was staring at Santa apprehensively and excitedly at the same time. His fingers were wiggling like worms, in that condescending way adults sometimes wave to little children when they're trying to be cute or they're uncomfortable with kids.

It apparently worked. The girl smiled shyly in return before waving back and looking at her feet. When she looked back up at Santa, he gestured for her to come to him. She looked tentatively up at her mother, who was still heatedly dealing with the security guard, beamed widely, and then took off across the mall. When she reached him, he knelt down and whispered in her ear. Her mouth dropped with excitement and she began bouncing in place as she nodded wildly. With each bounce, her golden pigtails flopped excitedly and danced off the back of her head.

Jack turned his attention back to the woman. The security guard reached for his radio and Jack heard the call on the radio at his hip.

Shoplifter in zone six, the voice called quickly. *Backup requested.*

This is it, Jack thought. He raised his radio to his lips, "319 to assist," he said, just as the paper in his pocket had instructed. He quickly crossed the distance between his hideout and the unfolding scene, and inserted himself into the situation. As he arrived, the security guard was removing a small bracelet from the woman's purse. He held it up at eye-level and inspected the woman accusingly. The woman's face displayed her surprise and she took a dramatic step back.

"What seems to be the problem?" Jack said, doing his best to act like a menial law enforcement official. The security guard eyed him with skepticism, but Jack knew in these types of situations, if he acted like he was in control, the man would be more than happy to relinquish it. He wasn't disappointed with the guard's reaction.

"I just found this in her bag," the guard said, holding up the bracelet for Jack to see.

"I have no idea how that got in there!" the woman objected loudly. "I swear. Just take it. I don't even want that ugly thing." She seemed genuinely upset, but did not display nervousness or fear.

Jack looked her up and down studying the situation. Her dark, shoulder length hair hung loosely, framing her face perfectly. Long, diamond earrings hung from her ears that matched her necklace and tennis bracelet. Her designer clothes hugged her frame snuggly, accentuating the parts she intended to advertise. Jack pegged her as a woman who was used to men doing what she said.

"Not quite how it works, ma'am," Jack returned curtly. "You've been caught shoplifting. We're going to have to hold you until the police get here and we can sort this out."

"You've got to be kidding me!" Her voice was escalating now. "I don't have to stand for this. I didn't steal that! Look at all the stuff I bought! Why would I pay for all of this and steal one little thing?" she said motioning to the other items in her bags.

"Let's take this conversation back into the store please, ma'am," Jack replied.

"Not a chance," she retorted quickly. "I'm leaving. You can't keep me here." She held her hand out behind her at waist level and snapped her fingers sharply. "Come on, Maddie. Let's go!"

When her daughter didn't respond or grab her hand, she wheeled around forcefully. "Maddie!" she was almost yelling.

"Ma'am, you can't leave," Jack said forcefully. Then he added, "Who's Maddie?" He did his best to fill his words with as much concern as he could muster.

"My daughter!" she replied, frantically searching the area for any sign of a puffy coat, pink poodle purse, or pigtails.

"Yeah," the security guard piped in, shaking his finger in the air. "There was a little girl here when I walked up." He began scanning the area as well. "She was wearing a big, puffy coat. What color was it ma'am?"

"Pink," the woman said; her voice cracking as she now attempted to fight back tears.

"What else was she wearing?" Jack asked, knowing full well.

"Blue jeans and…and a white shirt." She was noticeably upset. "And she had a little pink poodle hand bag." She was shaking as she began to cry and buried her hands in her face.

Jack brought the radio up to his lips. "We have a code Adam," he said before relaying the girl's description and their location. He was holding the stolen bracelet, and he quickly handed it back to the security guard who was still searching the area unsuccessfully. "No harm, no foul this time," he said nodding in the direction of the store. "Get this back where it goes, and I'll take her from here."

The security guard nodded to Jack in agreement, took the bracelet, and headed back into the store.

Like candy from a baby, Jack thought.

"What's your name, ma'am?" he asked the woman.

"Cynthia. Cynthia Knox," she said through sobs.

He took her hand and began walking toward the side hall he'd come from. "Don't worry, Cynthia. Your daughter's going to be fine. I promise. Come with me."

She took his hand and followed him. "Where are we going?"

"To get some help."

As they walked, Jack scanned the mall quickly. Before they turned down the hall toward the back of the mall, he caught a glimpse of a fat man in a red suit and hat turning a corner at the other end of the food court. Walking next to him was an elf in a green jacket and hat, holding a pink poodle purse, with blonde hair pulled back tightly into two neat pigtails.

The two new allies made their way to an exterior wall of the mall, ducking down a side corridor and behind a store. 'Mall Employees Only' signs greeted them as they sped through a pair of flimsy delivery doors and down a narrow service hallway.

"Where are we going?" she asked again absently, suddenly seeming more aware of her present surroundings.

"We're headed to the security hub of the mall," he replied definitively. "We have cameras there so we can see what happened to your daughter and find her if she's still in the mall."

She had slowed slightly, so Jack grabbed her arm forcefully and began pulling her along. She was resisting slightly, but Jack had to keep her feet moving in the same direction.

"I thought the security desk was at the front of the mall?" she said as she turned slightly away from Jack and pointed back in the direction they'd just come from.

"That's just the customer service security desk," he replied. "All the technology is back here.

They rounded a corner and were suddenly faced with two large double doors. Above the doors hung an exit sign. She eyed the doors skeptically as she stopped in her tracks. He still had a firm hold on her arm, but he could feel the tension as her arm tightened and she began to resist. He turned to face her, and they stood motionless for a moment.

"Are we going outside?" she asked looking at him from the tops of her eyes.

He grabbed her other arm just below the shoulder, tightened his grip, and leaned heavily on the door behind him, pulling her with him.

"Yep," he said as they spilled through the doorway and into the sunlight.

As soon as they stepped through the doorway, a black bag dropped over her face and she let out a muffled scream. The van that he'd arrived in was parked three feet from the door. Both of the cargo doors were propped open awaiting their arrival.

As she struggled to free herself, she lashed out behind her with her foot, catching Jack on his injured knee. He cursed loudly while the other assailant laughed at him. She continued to struggle, but even with the searing pain in his knee Jack was able to secure both her hands behind her while the other man snapped handcuffs into place. As she struggled, her thrashing gradually began to grow calmer and she began to teeter. Surprised by the change in her demeanor, Jack let go of her arms and watched as she stumbled awkwardly toward the van. Her knees began to buckle as she walked. She was passing out.

Jack took a step forward and grabbed her arms again steadying her. As he did, her head smacked his face and he became light-headed. Now he understood why she was fainting.

"Chloroform soaked hoodie," the man behind him chuckled callously. "Works every time." The man disgusted Jack. He would have just as soon killed him as worked with him.

It's just business, he reminded himself. He could make it personal later if he wanted.

Jack steadied himself while still holding the woman upright, slowly lowered her into the van, and removed the hood from her head.

"Looks like we have a goody-two-shoes," the brunette squawked from behind him. "Here you go, goody-two-shoes," she said throwing him his own hood and handcuffs. "Back on. We're out of here." She tossed the other man the same items and waited for them to put them on.

Once she was confident the men were secure, she slammed the doors behind them, and jumped back in the van. As Jack heard the door slam, the van lurched forward again and turned a corner. It stopped twice as it circled the mall to collect the other two men. Then it turned east, leaving the mall behind for good.

III

With the addition of a fifth body, the van's cargo area was even more cramped heading back the opposite direction. The woman's heavy perfume added to the smells of the compartment and a strong fuel smell was beginning to dominate the odors. Jack wondered offhandedly if they were trying to kill them all now that the job was done. He dismissed it quickly though. Honor among thieves and all that.

As the van rocked gently, Jack segregated himself in a corner, knees tucked into his chest to avoid contact with the other occupants. Once they'd left the city, the van traveled in a fairly straight line, reducing any movement by the newest, unconscious member.

After about thirty minutes, the van began to slow and pulled to the side of the road. Slamming doors were followed shortly by the cargo doors being pulled open once again. The sun had dropped lower into the sky and was streaming directly into the van's cabin. Even behind the hood, Jack had to once again squint against the new light pouring in.

The van rocked slightly as someone entered. Suddenly two strong hands grabbed his right arm and began dragging him to the door. The driver kicked and cursed at the men in his way as he dragged Jack toward the back of the van. He stepped down to the ground and then gave Jack one last tug, pulling him over the edge and dropping him roughly to the ground. Jack cursed under his breath.

I won't make it quick with you, he promised himself silently.

"On your knees, goody-two-shoes," the brunette called to him. He rocked himself up to a kneeling position, wincing at the pain in his knee as he did. It was stiffening more than he'd anticipated. When this was over, he was going to have to give the wound some attention.

Suddenly, the bag was ripped from his head and he squinted against the light that invaded his eyes. He rocked his head back and forth and closed his eyes tight in a futile attempt to fight the sun.

"Your fee," the brunette said as she tossed a small box in his direction. The box hit the ground hard, causing the lid to pop open. Through his squints, Jack could just make out the unmistakable green of cash peaking over the top of the side.

As his eyes slowly adjusted, he heard the two walk back toward the front of the van. The driver stepped into the van, but suddenly the footsteps from the brunette stopped and turned back in his direction. She stepped to his side and knelt down so close that her lips were almost touching his ear. He could feel her hot breath on his neck; could smell the cigarette stench from her mouth. He badly wanted a cigarette.

"I almost forgot," she whispered before dropping his revolver on the ground in front of him. Jack smiled at the sound of the metal clinking on the pebbles at his knees.

The brunette quickly turned back to the van and walked away.

"And what am I supposed to do with these?" he said shaking the handcuffs behind his back. As he shook them, his hands carefully reached for the tops of his socks and removed the two silver items he'd placed there an hour earlier.

"Not my problem, goody-two-shoes," she said over her shoulder as she continued to walk.

In one swift motion, Jack dropped his shoulders so his hands fell behind his feet. He rolled forward, slipping the handcuffs over his knees so they were now in front of him. He scooped up his revolver, and deftly slipped the two bullets into the cylinder. The brunette spun on her heels as she heard the quick sound on the gravel, but she was far too late. Through squinted eyes, Jack hammered her to the ground with one well-placed shot to the chest.

The driver, hearing the shot, grabbed his pistol and stepped back from the vehicle. Moving away from cover was his fatal mistake. As he turned, he presented a broad target and Jack delivered the second round to his stomach. The man screamed in agony and dropped to his knees, his weapon falling harmlessly to the dirt and out of his reach.

The men in the van were sitting up, quickly on alert with the commotion outside the vehicle. Their heads were waving back and forth in an attempt to find out what was going on. One of them began to stand up and edge his way to the back of the van. Another had rolled over, head down, and was slowly working at the bag as he pressed his face to the floor. All of them were yelling.

Jack quickly slammed the back doors of the van and made his way around the passenger side. Questioning screams and profanity erupted from the cargo area as the doors swung closed and latched into place. He opened the passenger door and grabbed the brunette's shotgun that was resting against the front seat. He eyed the driver through the open doors, who was now slumped in a ball on the ground, holding his stomach and groaning loudly.

He circled the front of the van and approached the man from behind. The man, although resigned to his fate, had regained some awareness and was slowly stretching toward his discarded weapon. Kicking the gun into the weeds, Jack pushed the man over onto his back with his foot and pointed the shotgun directly at the man's chest. Through shallow breaths, the man sneered at him, mocking him even at death's door.

"There was no need to be that mean," Jack said quietly. "If I had more time, I'd make you suffer. I should leave you alive for the buzzards."

The driver spit a curse that was barely audible through his labored breathing and groaning. Jack met his gaze only momentarily before pulling the trigger.

He dropped the shotgun to the ground next to the fresh corpse and looked up at the blue sky. He watched as a buzzard floated on the breeze, eyeing the buffet that was just laid out for him. He closed his eyes and took a deep breath. Muffled voices from inside the van permeated the shell as they questioned their fate and what had just happened. He studied the side of the vehicle out of the corner of his eye and then turned his attention to the box that had been tossed at his feet moments before. He walked over, picked up the box, and thumbed through the stack of cash. He counted ten 100-dollar bills before stopping. He didn't really care much about the money, but he wasn't going to let it rot with the corpses.

Tucking the stack of cash into his back pocket, he rounded the van to where the brunette lay. Digging through her pockets, he found the keys and finally removed the cuffs. He dropped them to the ground with a thud and massaged his wrists. Raising both arms to shoulder height and spreading his fingers, he arched his back and stretched forcefully, letting out a loud groan as he did. Shouts and more profanity were beginning to erupt from the back of the van, and he turned his attention to the commotion.

"Shut up or I'll kill you all!" he shouted into the openness around him. The voices stopped instantly, but he kept his attention trained on the side of the van for several more moments to see if he would have to follow up on his promise. He had no qualms with two of them, but the man with the chloroform hood could use killing.

When he was confident he wouldn't have to follow up, he once again knelt down by the brunette, this time searching her pockets for cigarettes and a lighter. Finding only a lighter, he stood back up, slammed the passenger door and circled the vehicle to the driver's side.

Half way into the driver seat, he stopped and looked down at his left foot. His gaze dropped from his shoe to the driver's feet. Sitting back down on the gravel, he put his shoe up to the bottom of the man's feet sizing them up. Once confident of the size, he made quick work of relieving the man of his now unnecessary attire, and laced them up tight, stretching his toes to their fullest in their new real estate. He rifled through the driver's pockets quickly for anything of importance, finding the cigarettes he was hoping for earlier.

He leaned hard against the van, lit a smoke, and inhaled deeply. The adrenaline rush was starting to wear off, and the nicotine was hitting his veins just at the right time. He slammed a hand hard against the side of the van to listen for a reaction. He heard nothing. He took his time finishing the cigarette, basking in the sunlight as it dipped lower in the sky, feeling the heat on his tired body.

With the hood finally gone for good, he took a moment to examine his knee. Rolling up his pant leg, he gingerly peeled the fabric away from the wound, leaving pieces of lint embedded in the gouge. It would need to be cleaned, and would probably require stitches, but at least it had stopped bleeding for now.

Taking one last long drag, he rolled his pant leg back down, put the cigarette out on the side of the van, and tossed the butt into the dirt on the side of the road. He picked up the shotgun from where he'd deposited it earlier and set it in the passenger seat. He climbed in and sat down on the worn seat, which squeaked its displeasure at him. Rolling down the window, he took one final look at the driver's face before slamming the van into drive.

He drove for ten minutes, taking several gravel roads and winding his way slowly back in the general direction of the city. After he'd put enough distance between him and the first stop, he pulled over to the side of the road and parked the van. He located the three boxes for the other men, and exited the van. He set the boxes on the ground several yards from the back of the van, and turned toward the vehicle.

The noise from the cargo area was starting to rise again as he stepped away from the boxes. He paused momentarily and then turned back, removing the cash from two of them, and tossing the empty boxes out of sight into the weeds. Shotgun in hand, he stepped to the back of the van and quickly opened the doors.

All three men jerked involuntarily as light poured into the cargo area yet again. The woman lay motionless, still unconscious. The smell of fetid urine and fresh vomit bowled him over as he surveyed the quartet. Apparently the sick man was still getting sick.

How much did that guy have to throw up? Jack thought angrily as he forcefully snorted outward.

"Up," he directed. All three slowly rolled to their feet and stood in the van apprehensively. "Get out," he said, keeping the shotgun trained on the group and backing away slowly. In unison the men crept to the edge of the cargo area, using their toes to feel for the ledge.

"What…what are you going to do with us?" the sick man finally mustered the courage to ask. Jack didn't answer. These scumbags didn't deserve an answer.

The chubby man had reached the back of the van and was still extending his foot to feel for the edge. As he swung his foot, one of the other men clambered out of the van, causing it to rock and the fat man lost his balance. He tumbled out of the back of the van and hit the ground hard, yelping loudly as he did. The woman stirred slightly. It was time to go.

"Take twenty steps and then turn around," Jack finally said, still ignoring their questions. Three heads jerked involuntarily and Jack knew they were still trying to decide if he was going to kill them too. He kicked the sick man in the butt.

"Move!" he yelled.

All three simultaneously took a tentative step forward, followed by another. Jack didn't wait to watch the rest. He quickly slammed the doors shut again, jumped in the driver seat and sped away, leaving the men looking around wildly beneath their hoods.

Jack didn't care what happened to them now. He didn't even care if they finished walking. Eventually one of them would get his hood off first, see the box of money, and try to kill the other two in an attempt to keep all the cash for himself.

The world will be better off, he thought as he drove.

This time he didn't take any winding roads or extra time. He made a straight line for town. The sun had almost set as Jack and his cargo reached their destination. He skirted along the city limits for several miles until he reached the commercial area, and pulled into the parking garage of a small warehouse.

Once parked, he stepped out of the van and pulled shut the overhead door of the garage. Somewhere in the distance he could hear a dog barking and its owner screaming at it to be quiet. He shook his head as the door slammed to the ground.

He moved to the van and opened the back doors slowly. The woman was just beginning to stir. He made his way around the passenger side to a table that sat along the garage wall. He picked up a handful of bullets from the table and loaded them into the cylinder of his revolver. Eyeing the sights down the length of the barrel, he squeezed off six shots, emptying the weapon. As he did, the woman came to and began screaming.

He stepped around to the back of the vehicle and watched as she tried futilely to sit up. She was searching back and forth with her head, frantically trying to gather her bearings or hear anything that would help her discern where she was or what was happening. He stepped up into the van and grabbed her roughly by the arm. She squirmed at his touch and screamed at him to get his hands off her. He dragged her to the edge of the cargo area and heaved her up over his shoulder. As he walked, she struggled in vain against his iron grip. They traversed two flights of steps and entered an upper room overlooking the garage. Once there, he dropped her into a chair and removed the blindfold.

"Do you recognize my face?" he asked her bluntly.

Her eyes adjusted to the light and she focused on his face. "You're the security guard from the mall," she said nodding and staring icy daggers through him. "Do you know who I am?" she replied indignantly.

"I do, Mrs. Knox," he replied calmly. "My name is Jack Stanton. I work for your husband. I was hired to kidnap and kill you."

IV

Jack watched her reaction closely as his words sunk in. Her understanding melted to disbelief before giving way to panic. She stared through the wall in front of her trying to sort it out. As she stared, Jack rounded the chair and deftly removed the handcuffs at her wrists. Finally realizing she was free, she looked up at him questioningly.

"Let me explain," he began trying to reassure her that she was safe for now. He softened his tone dramatically. "Do you know the name, William Mason?"

"No," she said, eyeing him apprehensively. She had brought her hands to chest level in front of her and was rubbing her wrists.

"Many years ago, he worked for Vincent." He watched her closely. Her eyes jumped at the sound of her husband's name. "He was in your home many times. Are you sure you don't know him?"

"I don't know the name," she confirmed resolutely.

"I doubt you'd recognize his face then," he said hopefully. She just stared at him.

He nodded his head slowly. "While he was working for your husband, William was also an undercover FBI agent."

She had looked down at the floor, but at the last comment she looked back up at him from the tops of her eyes and raised her eyebrows.

He continued. "William's real name was Anthony Turner. About eleven years ago, Vincent came by some information that an undercover agent was living in his city, but all he had was an address and a name; Anthony Turner. One night, he and a partner paid Mr. Turner a visit in his home. When they got there, they murdered him, his wife and their five-year-old daughter before burning their house to the ground."

Cynthia was now watching him intently. She leaned back in the chair chewing on her bottom lip. "What does this have to do with me?" she asked impatiently.

"The problem is, it wasn't Anthony Turner," Jack continued. "Anthony's brother was staying with them, and your husband unwittingly killed the wrong man. William was on the other side of town, pulling a job for your husband. Vincent didn't realize that William and Anthony were the same person until later."

"When Anthony found out his wife, daughter, and brother were all murdered, he went crazy and disappeared almost completely." Jack stopped and watched her momentarily to make sure the timeline of events was making sense. Confident she understood, he continued. "Because he worked for your husband as William, his sudden disappearance raised some eyebrows. Vincent sent me to find out what happened to him. His trail was pretty cold, but I just missed him two weeks later as he was crossing over into Mexico."

As he spoke, he crossed the room and dropped the handcuffs on a table that stood against a wall. Above the table was a window that overlooked the warehouse and the van parked in it. With the lights in the warehouse dimmed, it acted more as a mirror. He studied her face in the reflection. She was eyeing his back skeptically until she caught his eyes in the reflection and quickly became indignant.

"I still don't understand what this has to do with me now," she said defiantly.

Jack turned around, leaned against the table, and crossed his arms. "When I got back, I did a little digging on the man we thought was William Mason. I found out who he really was and what had happened. For the last eleven years, we've been keeping tabs on him. He never reported anything worthwhile to the FBI, so we've been perfectly content letting him rot in Mexico; far away from here. Vincent's drug interests in Mexico were far too valuable to jeopardize. He had no intention of following William into another country and creating a border war over someone we believed to be crazy." He paused intentionally at the end of his sentence.

She sat motionless for a moment before meeting his eyes again. "Believed?" she said catching his deliberate word choice.

He nodded slowly. "A week ago, we got word that he'd returned to the country. Two days after his return, a contract was put out on your head. We assume he's trying to get back at your husband by killing you."

She was looking nervous now. He could see that she was putting the pieces together. "Wait," she said suddenly, realization flickering in her eyes. "If he worked for the FBI, why aren't they looking for him?"

"They think he's dead," he replied matter-of-factly. "The house was burned to the ground. A week later, the FBI had a ceremony and buried what was left of the corpses they believed to be Anthony Turner and his family. He's been hiding in Mexico ever since."

"So," she said slowly. "If the FBI thought he was dead, how did you track him down?"

"Something didn't sit right with me. The FBI could have identified the bodies through dental records, so I knew he had to have someone helping him on the inside to falsify the evidence. I found that person, and beat him half to death until I got the truth." As he replied, he absently picked up a handful of bullets from the table and began reloading his pistol.

"And then what?"

"I beat the other half out of him." He rubbed his knuckles and paused to watch her reaction. She just blinked at him. "You're not scared of me?" he asked finally, displaying the gun for her to see clearly.

"You work for Vincent, yes?"

"Yes."

"Then, no. I'm not scared of you. If you touch a hair on my head, he'll skin you alive."

Jack chuckled under his breath and grinned. "Quite right," he said finally. He turned around and cupped his hand over his eyes so he could look down into the warehouse.

Finally Cynthia broke the silence. "So, how did you get yourself on the crew that kidnapped me?"

Jack snorted lightly as he turned back toward her. "Anthony was always smart, but he never had great judgment when it came to people he could trust. Like I said, we've been watching him from a distance. When it was clear he was coming back to the country, it was a pretty simple matter of picking up one of his stooges and coaxing the plan out of him. Once I knew the details, I got rid of the patsy and took his place on the highway."

Suddenly a thought struck her. "Where's my daughter?"

"Don't worry," he said quickly. "When mall security found her, they turned her over to the local authorities.

We needed her in a safe place for now. When this is done, we'll pick her up. We have a story prepared to cover your disappearance."

She was nodding slowly, taking it all in, apparently satisfied with that answer for the time being. "So, what now?"

"We wait." He looked at his watch quickly, readjusting the Velcro strap again. "Anthony believes that the kidnapping went off without a hitch, and is coming here personally to collect you soon. I'm going to kill whoever's with him and beat him senseless until your husband gets here at nine. Then we'll teach him the price of revenge."

He crossed the room to where she sat and handed her the pistol he'd just reloaded. She raised her hands hesitantly.

"Just in case," he said as she reluctantly took it from him.

He turned his back to her and walked back to the window to watch the warehouse. As he peered through the window, a flicker in the reflection caught his attention, drawing his line of sight upward. He focused on the source of the distraction only a second too late.

Behind him, Cynthia had leveled the gun at his back and was beginning to squeeze the trigger. Two shots rang through the silence as his body drove forward across the table into the glass. He slumped there breathing deeply for several tense moments, waiting for the rest of the gun to be emptied. Instead, it was her voice that broke the silence.

"You've had some work done, Anthony," she said with a hiss. "Your face is unrecognizable, but you couldn't change your eyes." As she ended her sentence, she emptied two more rounds into his back.

Through deep breaths, he finally replied slowly. "You know what's funny?" he said laughing at her. He looked up at her reflection and saw the hatred in her eyes. She didn't answer him.

"Most people don't use revolvers anymore," he said. "Back in the 80's, everyone wanted to be like Dirty Harry and carry a big magnum." He rolled over to look her in the eye. "Until they got into a gun fight and found out how useless six shots really are." He stood up from the table to face her, removing another pistol from under his shirt and leveling it at her chest.

As he spoke, the fear in her eyes betrayed her realization that something was wrong. She aimed the gun at his face and pulled the trigger again, but only an audible click was produced this time. She fired the weapon repeatedly, with increasing animation before discarding the useless hunk of metal by hurling it to the floor.

He continued. "On the other hand, when you're breaking into someone's house and they're not expecting you, a revolver works just fine." She was backing away slowly now. "The FBI never did find the gun that killed my family," he said slowly. "But I did." He looked down at the gun and then back up to her face, staring straight into her eyes. "And I found Vincent's partner, too."

She began to fan out her hands, reaching for anything that would help her. "You were clever," he continued. "It took me eleven years to piece it together, but you've been behind everything from the beginning haven't you? Your husband's not running the organization, is he? You are. It was you who got the tip that I was in town, and it was your idea to murder me and burn my house to the ground. You sent the gun back to your hometown in Mexico. I chased Vincent's past for years until I realized the truth. I should have been chasing yours."

Suddenly her demeanor changed. She straightened herself, becoming much less prey and taking on the look of the hunter. A wicked smile curled her upper lip and she practically snarled at him. "You have no idea what you're dealing with," she hissed at him. "You think I'm going down without a fight? My husband will hunt you down like a dog. You won't be safe anywhere."

"You mean the husband that was just shot downstairs with that gun?" he said, nodding to the now-discarded revolver that lay on the floor. "Thank you for putting your fingerprints on it."

She looked at him and squinted, studying him intently.

"You knew me as William," he said breaking the silence. "So did your husband. Too bad he wasn't smart enough to see through the lies I told him to get him here. It cost him his life."

"I will end yours," she replied coldly. "This time you won't be safe in Mexico. I'll hunt you to the end of the earth." Her voice was shrill; cold and filled with malice. Her eyes sparkled even in the dim light.

"You'll have to get out of jail first," he replied quietly. "Oh," he continued, "and don't worry about your daughter. I told you the police have her, and they do. But they'll be all too willing to turn her over to the FBI officer that's been working this case for eleven years." He paused for a moment, reflecting. "My daughter was five when you took her from me. About the same age as your daughter is now. I'll give her a better life than you ever would have."

At the last words, she screamed and hurled herself at him, trying desperately to cross the distance between them. He fired a warning shot at her feet, but she kept coming. Side-stepping her wild assault, he tripped her, sending her sprawling hard into the legs of the table behind him.

Muffled voices were coming from the garage as footsteps began to climb the two flights of stairs leading to the room. She rolled over, pushing the table off her and cursing at him, but now fixed her attention on the door.

As she momentarily sat motionless, Jack picked up a jacket from a nearby stool, and quickly slipped it on. He kept the pistol trained on her the entire time. Cynthia's eyes moved from the door back to Jack. Her eyes fixed intensely on the police star on his chest as he zipped up the jacket and slowly backed to the door behind him. As he exited, the door on the opposite side of the room burst open and two police officers erupted into view, pistols drawn.

"Hands behind your head, ma'am," the first officer said as he approached her.

She stood slowly, lips curled at the officers as they brought her hands to her head. The warmth from the officer's grip gave way to the cold metal of the handcuffs. She jumped slightly as they clicked into place.

"There it is," a third man said, entering the room and pointing at the revolver on the ground. "Just like he said."

"You think that's really the gun that killed the Turner family?" one of the officers asked.

"We're going to find out," the third man replied, picking up the weapon with a rag and depositing it into a plastic bag. "I'm assuming it's the weapon that killed the man downstairs too." He eyed it thoughtfully and shook his head. He wasn't letting this weapon out of his sight.

Then he turned his attention to their new prisoner. "Mrs. Knox, my name is Jack Stanton. I'm with the FBI. These boys are going to read you your rights, and then we're going to go downtown and have a long conversation."

ABOUT THE AUTHOR

Robert Palmer resides in Sioux Falls, SD with his wife and two of his four amazing children. He is an avid golfer, writer, football fan, father, and husband.

CPSIA information can be obtained
at www.ICGtesting.com
Printed in the USA
LVHW022131080520
655244LV00002B/728